Reader's Digest

BEST LOVED BOOKS
FOR YOUNG READERS

The Merry
Adventures of
Robin Hood

A CONDENSATION OF THE BOOK BY

Howard Pyle

Illustrated by Jean Leon Huens

CHOICE PUBLISHING, INC.

New York

PRODUCED IN ASSOCIATION WITH MEDIA PROJECTS INCORPORATED

Executive Editor, Carter Smith
Managing Editor, Jeanette Mall
Project Editor, Jacqueline Ogburn
Associate Editor, Charles Wills
Contributing Editor, Elizabeth Prince
Art Director, Bernard Schleifer

Library of Congress Catalog Number: 88-63352
ISBN: 0-945260-20-2

This 1989 edition is published and distributed by Choice Publishing, Inc.,
Great Neck, NY 11021, with permission of The Reader's Digest Association, Inc.

Manufactured in the United States of America.

10 9 8 7 6 5 4 3 2

Foreword

IN THE ENGLAND OF the Middle Ages many a daring tale was told, many a romantic ballad sung about Robin Hood—the gallant outlaw who stole boldly from the rich that he might give generously to the poor. Like King Arthur, he is a legendary figure. But whereas Arthur was a hero of the knightly classes, Robin was the beloved champion of the peasantry.

Howard Pyle has chosen the best of the Robin Hood stories for this book. He has placed Robin in the twelfth century during the successive reigns of Henry II with his beautiful queen, Eleanor of Aquitaine, and their chivalrous son, Richard the Lion-Hearted, and of Richard's tyrannical brother, John. This was a time when the land was tilled by Saxon serfs but owned by Norman noblemen and wealthy churchmen. The forests, which abounded in game, were royal property, with heavy penalties for poaching therein, even when famine stalked the countryside. The common folk were often oppressed, and it was only natural that they should dream of a hero of their very own—a young man who freely roamed the forests, who laughed merrily at the hated authorities, who revered God but played pranks on pompous clergymen.

Whether Robin was real, imaginary, or a composite of several men, no one knows. But Sherwood Forest in Nottingham was—and is—a real place. Much of it has been destroyed to make room for farms and factories, but part of it has been preserved. Here the sunlight still filters through great trees to fall on grassy glades, and one can almost hear the call of Robin's horn, and the twang of his bowstring in the leafy quiet. Here, as in the pages of Howard Pyle's book, he seems very much alive.

Howard Pyle also wrote and illustrated *The Story of King Arthur and His Knights*, *Otto of the Silver Hand*, and *Men of Iron*. Born in Wilmington, Delaware, in 1853, he attended school there and began to study art while helping his father in the leather business. Later he devoted all his time to writing, painting, and teaching. In 1900 he started an art school, and his pupils included many who later became famous, such as N. C. Wyeth and Maxfield Parrish. He died in 1911.

How
Robin Hood
Came
to Be an
Outlaw

IN MERRY ENGLAND in the time of old, when good King Henry the Second ruled the land, there lived within the green glades of Sherwood Forest, near Nottingham Town, a famous outlaw whose name was Robin Hood. No archer ever lived that could speed a shaft with such skill as his, nor were there ever such yeomen as the sevenscore merry men that roamed with him through the greenwood, passing their time in games of archery or bouts of cudgel play, and living upon the King's venison washed down with draughts of ale. Not only Robin himself but all the band were outlaws and dwelt apart from other men, yet they were beloved by the country people round about, for no one ever came to jolly Robin for help in time of need and went away with an empty fist.

And now I will tell how it came about that Robin Hood fell afoul of the law.

When Robin was a youth of eighteen, stout of sinew and bold of heart, the Sheriff of Nottingham proclaimed a shooting match and offered a prize of a butt of ale to whosoever should shoot the best shaft in Nottinghamshire. "Now," quoth Robin, "will I go too, for fain would I draw a string for a butt of good October brewing." So he took his good stout yew bow and a score of broad cloth-yard arrows, and started off from his home in Locksley Town through Sherwood Forest to Nottingham.

It was at the dawn of day in the merry Maytime, when hedge-rows are green and flowers bedeck the meadows; when apple buds blossom and birds sing, the lark, the throstle cock and cuckoo; when lads and lasses look upon each other with sweet thoughts; when housewives spread their linen to bleach upon the grass. Sweet was the greenwood, and blithely Robin whistled as he trudged along its paths.

Suddenly he came upon some foresters beneath a great oak tree. Fifteen there were in all, feasting and drinking as they sat around a huge pasty, each thrusting his hands into the pie and washing down that which he ate with great horns of ale. Then one of them, with his mouth full, called out to Robin, "Halloa, where goest thou, little lad, with thy one-penny bow and thy farthing shafts?"

Then Robin grew angry, for no stripling likes to be taunted with his green years. "Now," quoth he, "my bow and mine arrows are as good as thine. I go to the shooting match at Nottingham Town."

"Ho! Listen to the lad!" said one. "Why, boy, thy mother's milk is yet scarce dry upon thy lips, and yet thou pratest of standing up with good stout men at Nottingham butts."

"I'll hold you twenty marks," quoth Robin, "that I hit the clout at threescore rods."

Then all laughed aloud, and one said, "Well boasted, thou fair infant, well boasted! And well thou knowest that no target is nigh to make good thy wager."

At this Robin grew right mad. "Hark ye," said he, "yonder, at the glade's end, I see a herd of deer, even more than threescore rods distant. I'll hold you twenty marks that, by leave of Our Lady, I cause the best hart among them to die."

"Now done!" cried he who had spoken first. "I wager that thou causest no beast to die, with or without the aid of Our Lady."

Then Robin took his bow in his hand, and placing the tip at his instep he strung it right deftly; then he nocked an arrow and, raising the bow, drew the gray goose feather to his ear; the next moment the bowstring rang and the arrow sped down the glade as a sparrow hawk skims in a northern wind. High leaped the noblest hart of all the herd, only to fall dead on the path.

"Ha!" cried Robin. "How likest thou that shot, good fellow?"

Then all the foresters were filled with rage, and he who had lost the wager was more angry than all. "Knowest thou not," cried he, "that thou hast killed the King's deer, and, by the laws of King Harry, thine ears should be shaven close to thy head?"

Never a word said Robin Hood, but he looked at the foresters with a grim face; then, turning on his heel, he strode away from them down the forest glade.

Now, he who had first spoken sprang to his feet and seized upon his bow. "I'll hurry thee anon," cried he. And he sent an arrow whistling after Robin.

It was well for Robin that the forester's head was spinning with ale, or else he would never have taken another step. As it was, the arrow whistled within three inches of his head. Then he turned and quickly drew his own bow, and sent an arrow in return. "Ye said I was no archer," cried he, "but say so now again!"

The shaft flew straight; the archer fell forward with a cry and lay on his face upon the ground, his arrows rattling about him from out of his quiver, the gray goose shaft wet with his heart's blood. Then Robin Hood was gone into the depths of the green-wood. Some started after him, but not with much heart, for each feared to suffer the death of his fellow; so presently they all came back and bore the dead man away to Nottingham.

Meanwhile Robin ran through the greenwood. Gone was all the joy and brightness, for his heart was sick. "Alas," cried he, "I would that my right forefinger had been stricken off ere this had happened. In haste I smote, but grieve I sore at leisure."

And so he came to dwell in the greenwood, never again to see the happy days with the lads and lasses of Locksley Town. For he was outlawed: he had killed a man, and he had poached upon the King's deer, and two hundred pounds were set upon his head.

Now the Sheriff of Nottingham swore that he himself would bring this knave to justice; first, because he wanted the two hundred pounds, and next, because the forester that Robin Hood had killed was of kin to him. But Robin hid in Sherwood Forest, and there gathered around him many others like himself. Some had shot deer in hungry wintertime, when they could get no other food, and had been seen in the act by the foresters, but had escaped; some had been turned out of their inheritance, that their farms might be added to the King's lands; some had been despoiled by a great baron or a rich abbot.

So, in one year, fivescore or more good stout yeomen gathered about Robin Hood, and chose him to be their chief. They vowed that even as they themselves had been despoiled they would despoil their oppressors, and that from each they would take that which had been wrung from the poor by unjust taxes, or in wrongful fines. But to the poor folk they would give help in need and trouble. Besides this, they swore never to harm a child nor to wrong a woman; so that, after a while, the people came to praise Robin and his men, and to tell many tales of him and of his doings.

ONE MORN WHEN ALL THE BIRDS were singing blithely among the leaves, up rose Robin Hood and all his merry men, each washing his head and hands in the brook that leaped laughing from stone to stone. Then said Robin, "Today I will go abroad to seek adventures. But tarry ye all in the greenwood; only see that ye mind well my call. Three blasts upon the bugle horn I will blow in my hour of need; then come quickly, for I shall want your aid."

So saying, he strode away through the leafy forest glades until he had come to the verge of Sherwood. There he wandered through highway and byway. Now he met a buxom lass in a shady lane, and each gave the other a merry word and passed his way; now he saw a fair lady upon an ambling pad, to whom he doffed his cap, and who bowed sedately in return; now he saw a fat monk on a pannier-laden ass; now a gallant knight, with spear and shield and armor that flashed brightly in the sunlight; and now a stout burgher from Nottingham Town, pacing along with serious footsteps; but adventure he found none. At last he took a bypath that dipped toward a broad, pebbly stream spanned by a narrow bridge made of a log of wood. As he drew nigh this bridge he saw a tall stranger coming from the other side. Thereupon Robin quickened his pace, as did the stranger, each thinking to cross first.

"Now stand thou back," quoth Robin, "and let the better man cross first."

"Nay," answered the stranger, "then stand back thine own self, for the better man, I wot, am I."

"Stand thou," quoth Robin, "or else, by the bright brow of Saint Ælfrida, I will show thee right good Nottingham play with a cloth-yard shaft betwixt thy ribs."

"Thou pratest like a coward," answered the stranger. "Thou standest there with a bow, while I have naught but a staff."

"By my faith," quoth Robin. "Never have I had a coward's name. I will lay by my bow, and if thou darest abide my coming, I will go and cut a cudgel to test thy manhood withal."

"Aye, marry, that will I abide and joyously," quoth the stranger.

Then Robin Hood stepped quickly to the coverside and cut a staff of ground oak, straight, without flaw, and six feet in length, and came back trimming away the tender stems from it, while the stranger leaned upon his staff and whistled as he gazed round about. Robin observed him furtively as he trimmed his staff, measuring him from top to toe from out the corner of his eye, and thought that he had never seen a stouter man. Tall was Robin, but taller was the stranger by a head, for he was seven feet in height. Broad was Robin across the shoulders, but broader was the stranger by twice the breadth of a palm.

Nevertheless, said Robin to himself, I will baste thy hide, my good fellow. Then aloud, "Lo, here is my staff. Now meet an thou darest. We will fight until one of us tumble into the stream by dint of blows."

"Marry, that meeteth my whole heart!" cried the stranger, twirling his staff above his head betwixt his fingers and thumb.

Never did the knights of Arthur's Round Table meet in a stouter fight than did these two. Robin stepped quickly upon the bridge where the stranger stood; first he made a feint, and then delivered a blow at the stranger's head that, had it met its mark, would have tumbled him speedily into the water. But the stranger turned the blow right deftly and in return gave one as stout, which Robin also turned. So they stood, each in his place, neither moving

5

a finger's breadth back, for one good hour, and many blows were given and received, till here and there were sore bones and bumps, yet neither thought of crying "Enough," or seemed likely to fall from off the bridge. At last Robin gave the stranger a blow that made his jacket smoke like a damp straw thatch in the sun; but he regained himself right quickly and thwacked Robin so fairly that he fell heels over head into the water.

"And where art thou now, my good lad?" shouted the stranger, roaring with laughter.

"Oh, floating adown with the tide," cried Robin, nor could he forbear laughing himself at his sorry plight. He waded to the bank, the little fish speeding hither and thither, all frightened at his splashing. "Give me thy hand. I must needs own thou art a brave soul and a good one with the cudgels. My head hummeth like to a hive of bees." Then he clapped his horn to his lips and winded three blasts that went echoing down the forest paths.

"And thou," quoth the stranger, "takest thy cudgeling like a stout yeoman."

But now the distant twigs and branches rustled, and suddenly a score or two of men, all clad in Lincoln green, burst from out the covert, with Will Stutely at their head.

"Good master," cried Will, "how is this? Truly thou art all wet from head to foot, and that to the very skin."

"Why, marry," answered Robin, "yon stout fellow hath tumbled me into the water and given me a drubbing besides."

"Then shall he not go without a ducking and a drubbing himself!" cried Will Stutely. "Have at him, lads!"

Then the yeomen leaped upon the stranger, but they found him ready and felt him strike right and left with his staff, so that, though he went down with press of numbers, some of them rubbed cracked crowns before he was overcome.

"Nay, forbear!" cried Robin, laughing until his sore sides ached again. "He is a right good man and true. Now hark ye, good youth, wilt thou be one of my band? Three suits of Lincoln green shalt thou have each year, and share with us whatsoever good shall befall us. Thou shalt eat sweet venison and quaff the stoutest ale, and mine own good right-hand man shalt thou be, for never did I see such a cudgel player in all my life before."

"That know I not," quoth the stranger surlily, for he was angry at being so tumbled about, "if ye handle yew bow no better than ye do oaken cudgel; but if there be any man here that can shoot a better shaft than I, then will I join with you."

"Now by my faith," said Robin, "thou art a saucy varlet. Good Stutely, cut thou a white piece of bark four fingers in breadth, and set it fourscore yards distant on yonder oak. Now, stranger, hit that with a gray goose shaft and call thyself an archer."

"Aye, marry, that will I," answered he. "And if I hit it not, strip me and beat me blue with bowstrings."

Then he chose the stoutest bow among them all, next to Robin's own, and a straight shaft, well feathered and smooth, and, stepping to the mark, drew the arrow to his cheek and loosed the shaft right deftly, sending it so straight that it clove the mark in the very center. "Aha!" cried he. "Mend thou that if thou canst," while even the yeomen clapped at so fair a shot.

"That is a keen shot indeed," quoth Robin. "Mend it I cannot, but mar it I may, perhaps." Then taking up his own stout bow, he shot with his greatest skill. So true flew the arrow that it lit fairly upon the stranger's shaft and split it into splinters.

"By the lusty yew bow of good Saint Withold," cried the stranger, "never saw I the like! Now truly will I be thy man."

"Then have I gained a right good man this day," quoth jolly Robin. "What name goest thou by, good fellow?"

"Men call me John Little whence I came," answered the stranger.

Then Will Stutely, who loved a jest, spoke up. "Nay, fair stranger, little art thou indeed, and small of bone and sinew, therefore shalt thou be christened Little John."

Then all the band laughed until the stranger grew angry. "An thou make a jest of me," quoth he, "thou wilt have sore bones."

"Nay, good friend," said Robin Hood, "bottle thine anger, for the name fitteth thee well. So come, my merry men, we will prepare a christening feast for this fair infant."

So through the forest they traced their steps till they reached the spot where they dwelt. There had they built huts of bark and branches of trees, and made couches of sweet rushes spread over with skins of fallow deer. Here stood a great oak tree with branches spreading broadly around, beneath which was a seat of green moss where Robin Hood was wont to sit. Here they found the rest of the band, some of whom had come in with a brace of fat does. They built great fires and roasted the does and broached a barrel of humming ale. Then they all sat down, but Robin placed Little John at his right hand, for he was henceforth to be the second in the band.

When the feast was done Will Stutely spoke up. "It is now time, I ween, to christen our bonny babe. Seven sponsors shall we have." And he chose the seven stoutest men, and together they ran upon Little John, seizing him by his legs and arms and holding him tightly in spite of his struggles. Then one came forward who had been chosen to play the priest because he had a bald crown. "Now, what name callest thou this babe?" asked he right soberly.

"Little John call I him," answered Will Stutely.

"Now Little John," quoth the mock priest, "thou hast not lived heretofore, but henceforth thou wilt live indeed. When thou lived not thou wast called John Little, but now that thou dost live, Little John shalt thou be called, so christen I thee." And at these words he emptied a pot of ale upon Little John's head. Then all shouted with laughter as the ale trickled from his nose and beard, his eyes blinked with the smart of it, and he too laughed. Then Robin clothed him from top to toe in Lincoln green, and gave him a good stout bow, and so made him a member of the band.

The Shooting Match at Nottingham Town

NOW IT WAS TOLD BEFORE how two hundred pounds were set upon Robin Hood's head, and how the Sheriff of Nottingham swore that he would seize Robin. Now the Sheriff did not know what a force Robin had about him, but thought that he might serve a warrant as he could upon any other man that had broken the laws; therefore he offered fourscore golden angels to anyone who would serve this warrant. But men of Nottingham Town knew more of Robin than the Sheriff did, and laughed to think of serving a warrant upon the bold outlaw. So a fortnight passed, in which time none came forward to do the Sheriff's business.

Then it came to the Sheriff's ears that the people made a jest of him, and he was very wroth, because a man hates nothing so much as being made a jest of. Not a word did the Sheriff speak to anyone, but all the time he was devising a plan to take Robin Hood.

Then of a sudden it came to him that were he to proclaim a great shooting match and offer some grand prize, Robin Hood might be overpersuaded by his spirit to come to the butts, even within the walls of Nottingham Town; and the Sheriff cried, "Aha!" and smote his palm upon his thigh.

So he sent messengers north and south, and east and west, to proclaim through town, hamlet and countryside this grand shooting match, and the prize was to be an arrow of pure beaten gold.

When Robin Hood first heard this news he called his men about him and spoke to them thus: "Now hearken all. Our friend the Sheriff of Nottingham hath proclaimed a shooting match, and the prize is to be a bright golden arrow. Now I fain would have one of us win it, both because of the fairness of the prize and because our friend the Sheriff hath offered it. What say ye, lads?"

Then young David of Doncaster spoke up and said, "I have come straight from our friend Eadom o' the Blue Boar Inn, good master, and there I heard that the Sheriff hath but laid a trap for thee in this match. So go not lest we all meet dole and woe."

"Now," quoth Robin, "thou art a wise lad and keepest thine ears open, as becometh a crafty woodsman. But shall we let it be said that the Sheriff did cow bold Robin Hood and sevenscore as fair archers as are in all England? Nay, good David, what thou tellest me maketh me desire the prize even more. But we must meet guile with guile. Now some of you clothe yourselves as friars, and some as peasants, and some as tinkers, but see that each man taketh a good bow or broadsword, in case need should arise. As for myself, I will shoot for this golden arrow, and should I win it, we will hang it to the branches of our greenwood tree."

Then, "Good, good!" cried all the band right heartily.

A fair sight was Nottingham Town on the day of the shooting match. All along the meadow beneath the town wall stretched a row of benches, one above the other, which were for knight and lady, squire and dame, and rich burghers and their wives. The range was twoscore paces broad, and sevenscore and ten paces in length. At one end, near the target, was a raised seat, bedecked with ribbons and garlands, for the Sheriff of Nottingham and his dame; at the other a tent of striped canvas, from the pole of which fluttered many colored flags and streamers.

Already, while it was early, the benches were beginning to fill, the people arriving in little carts or upon palfreys that curvetted gaily to the tinkle of silver bells at bridle reins. With these came also the poorer folk, who sat or lay upon the grass behind a railing. In the great tent the archers were gathering, some talking loudly of the fair shots each man had made in his day, some looking well to their bows, drawing a string betwixt the fingers to see that there was no fray upon it, or peering down a shaft to see that it was straight and true. And never was such a company of yeomen as had come to this shooting match. There was Gill o' the Red Cap, the Sheriff's own head archer, and Diccon Cruikshank of Lincoln Town, and Adam o' the Dell, a man of Tamworth, of threescore years and more, yet hale and lusty still, and many more.

At last the Sheriff came with his lady, he riding with stately mien upon his milk-white horse and she upon her brown filly. He wore a purple velvet cap, and purple velvet was his robe, all trimmed with ermine; his jerkin and hose were of sea-green silk, and his shoes of black velvet, the pointed toes fastened to his garters with golden chains. A golden chain hung about his neck, and at his collar was a great carbuncle set in red gold. His lady was in blue velvet, all trimmed with swansdown. And so they came to their place, where men-at-arms in chain mail awaited them.

Then the Sheriff bade his herald wind upon his silver horn, who thereupon sounded three blasts that came echoing back from the walls of Nottingham. The archers stepped to their places, while all the folks shouted with a mighty voice, each man calling upon his favorite. "Red Cap!" "Cruikshank!" "Hey for William o' Leslie!" And the ladies waved silken scarfs to urge each yeoman to do his best.

Then the Sheriff leaned forward, looking keenly among the archers to find whether Robin Hood was among them; but no one was there clad in Lincoln green. Nevertheless, said the Sheriff to himself, he may still be there among the crowd. Let me see when the ten best men shoot, for I wot he will be among them.

And now the archers shot, one arrow each in turn, and the good folk never saw such archery as was done that day. Then ten men were chosen of all those that had shot before, and of these, six were famous throughout the land: Gilbert o' the Red Cap, Adam o' the Dell, Diccon Cruikshank, William o' Leslie, Hubert o' Cloud and Swithin o' Hertford. Two others were yeomen of Yorkshire, another was a stranger in blue, who said he came from London Town, and the last was a tattered stranger in scarlet, who wore a patch over one eye.

"Now," quoth the Sheriff to a man-at-arms who stood near him, "see'st thou Robin Hood among those ten?"

"Nay, your worship," answered the man. "Six of them I know right well. Of those Yorkshire yeomen, one is too tall and the other too short for that bold knave. Robin's beard is as yellow as gold, while yon beggar in scarlet hath a beard of brown, besides being blind of one eye. As for the stranger in blue, Robin's shoulders, I ween, are three inches broader than his."

"Then," quoth the Sheriff, smiting his thigh angrily, "yon knave is a coward as well as a rogue, and dares not show his face."

Then those ten stepped forth to shoot again. Each shot two arrows, and all the crowd watched with scarce a sound; but when the last had shot a great shout arose for such marvelous shooting.

And now but three men were left. One was Gill o' the Red Cap, one the tattered stranger in scarlet, and one Adam o' the Dell. Then some of the people called aloud, "Ho for Gilbert o' the Red Cap!" and some, "Hey for stout Adam o' Tamworth!" But not a single man called upon the stranger in scarlet.

First to shoot was Gill o' the Red Cap. Straight flew his arrow and lit fairly in the clout, a finger's breadth from the center. "A

Gilbert, a Gilbert!" shouted the crowd. And, "Now, by my faith," cried the Sheriff, smiting his hands together, "that is a shrewd shot."

Then the tattered stranger stepped forth, and all the people laughed as they saw a yellow patch that showed beneath his arm when he raised his elbow to shoot. He drew the good yew bow quickly, and so quickly loosed a shaft that no man could draw a breath betwixt the drawing and the shooting; yet his arrow lodged nearer the center than the other by twice the length of a barleycorn.

"Now by all the saints in paradise!" cried the Sheriff. "That is a lovely shaft in very truth!"

Adam o' the Dell shot, carefully and cautiously, and his arrow lodged close beside the stranger's. Then after a short space they all three shot again, and once more each arrow lodged within the clout, and again the stranger's shot was the best. And after another time of rest, they all shot for the third time. Gilbert took great heed to his aim. Straight flew the arrow, and all shouted till the very flags shook with the sound, for the shaft lodged close beside the spot that marked the center.

"Well done, Gilbert!" cried the Sheriff joyously. "Now, thou ragged knave, let me see thee shoot a better shaft than that."

Naught spoke the stranger but took his place, holding his bow in his hand while one could count five; then he drew his trusty yew, holding it drawn but a moment, then loosed the string. So true flew the arrow that it smote a gray goose feather from off Gilbert's shaft, which fell fluttering through the sunlit air as the stranger's arrow lodged close beside his of the Red Cap, and in the very center. And no one shouted, but each looked into his neighbor's face amazedly.

"Nay," quoth old Adam o' the Dell, drawing a long breath and shaking his head, "twoscore years and more have I shot shaft, and maybe not all times bad, but I shoot no more this day, for no man can match with yon stranger, whosoe'er he may be."

Then the Sheriff came down from his dais and drew near to where the stranger stood, while the folk crowded around to see the man who shot so wondrously well. "Here, good fellow," quoth the Sheriff, "take thou the prize, and fairly hast thou won it. What may be thy name, and whence comest thou?"

"Men do call me Jock o' Teviotdale," said the stranger.

"Then, by Our Lady, Jock, thou art the fairest archer that e'er mine eyes beheld. I trow thou drawest better bow than that same coward knave Robin Hood, that dared not show his face here this day. Say, good fellow, wilt thou join my service? I will clothe thee with a better coat than that thou hast upon thy back, and at every Christmastide fourscore marks shall be thy wage."

"Nay," quoth the stranger roughly. "I will be mine own, and no man in all England shall be my master."

"Then get thee gone, and a murrain seize thee!" cried the Sheriff, and his voice trembled with anger. "By my faith, I have a good part of a mind to have thee beaten for thine insolence!" Then he turned upon his heel and strode away.

It was a motley company that gathered about the greenwood tree in Sherwood that same day: a score of barefoot friars, and some that looked like tinkers, and some that seemed to be rustic hinds. And on a mossy couch was one clad in tattered scarlet, with a patch over one eye; and in his hand he held a golden arrow. Then, amid the talking and laughter, he took the patch from his eye and stripped the rags from his body and showed himself all clothed in Lincoln green; and quoth he, "Easy come these things away, but walnut stain cometh not so speedily from yellow hair." Then all laughed louder than before, for it was Robin himself.

Then all sat down to the woodland feast and talked of the jest that had been played upon the Sheriff. But when the feast was done, Robin took Little John apart and said, "Truly am I vexed in my blood, for I heard the Sheriff say today, 'Thou drawest better bow than that coward knave Robin Hood.' I would fain let him know who it was who won the golden arrow from out his hand."

Then Little John said, "Good master, take thou me and Will Stutely, and we will send yon fat Sheriff news of all this by a messenger such as he doth not expect."

That day the Sheriff sat at meat in the great hall of his house at Nottingham Town. Long tables stood down the hall, at which sat men-at-arms and household servants, in all fourscore and more.

The Sheriff sat at the head of the table upon a raised seat under a canopy, and beside him sat his dame. "By my troth," said he, "who could that saucy knave be who answered me so bravely? I wonder that I did not have him beaten; but there was something about him that spoke of other things than rags and tatters."

Even as he finished speaking, something fell rattling among the dishes on the table, startling those that sat near. It was a blunted gray goose shaft, which had been shot through the window, with a fine scroll tied near to its head. The Sheriff opened the scroll and read it, while the veins upon his forehead swelled and his cheeks grew ruddy with rage, for this was what he saw:

> *Now heaven bless thy Grace this day,*
> *Say all in sweet Sherwood,*
> *For thou didst give the prize away*
> *To merry Robin Hood.*

Will Stutely Rescued by His Companions

Now when the Sheriff found that neither law nor guile could overcome Robin Hood, he was much perplexed, and said to himself, I will try what may be done with might.

So he called his constables together. "Now take ye each four men, all armed in proof," said he, "and get ye to the forest, at different points, and lie in wait. To him that first meeteth with Robin Hood shall one hundred pounds of silver money be given if he be brought to me dead or alive; and to him that meeteth with any of his band shall twoscore pounds be given if such be brought to me."

So they went in threescore companies of five to Sherwood Forest, to take Robin Hood. For seven days they hunted, but never saw so much as a single man in Lincoln green; for tidings of all this had been brought to Robin Hood by trusty Eadom o' the Blue Boar, and Robin had said, "If the Sheriff dare send force to meet force, blood will flow. But fain would I not deal sorrow to women-folk and wives because good stout yeomen lose their lives. Once I slew a man, and never do I wish to slay a man again."

So Robin and his men hid in the depths of Sherwood for seven days; but early on the eighth day Robin Hood said to Will Stutely, "Now go you and find what the Sheriff's men are at. For I know right well they will not bide forever within Sherwood shades."

Then Will Stutely clad himself in a friar's gown, and underneath the robe he hung a good broadsword. Thus clad, he set forth, until he came to the Sign of the Blue Boar. For, quoth he to himself, our good friend Eadom will tell me all the news.

Now no sweeter inn could be found in all Nottinghamshire than the Blue Boar. None had such lovely trees standing around, or was so covered with trailing clematis and woodbine; none had such good beer; nor, in wintertime, when the north wind howled and snow drifted around the hedges, was there to be found such a roaring fire as blazed upon the hearth. There had Robin Hood and his merry companions often gathered. As for mine host, he knew how to keep a still tongue in his head, for he knew very well which side of his bread was spread with butter, for Robin and his men were the best of customers and paid their scores without having them chalked up behind the door.

Here Will Stutely found a band of the Sheriff's men drinking right lustily. He sat down upon a distant bench, his staff in his hand, and his head bowed as though he were meditating, until he might see the landlord apart. As Stutely sat thus, a house cat came and rubbed against his knee, raising his robe a palm's breadth high. Stutely pushed his robe quickly down again, but the constable who commanded the Sheriff's men saw fair Lincoln green beneath the friar's robe. Yon is no friar of orders gray, he said to himself; and also, I wot, no honest yeoman goeth about in priest's garb. Now I think in good sooth that is one of Robin Hood's own men. So, presently, he said aloud, "Whither goest thou, holy friar?"

"I go a pilgrim to Canterbury Town," answered Will Stutely, speaking gruffly, so that none might know his voice.

Then the constable said, "Now tell me, holy father, do pilgrims to Canterbury wear Lincoln green beneath their robes?" And he flashed forth his bright sword and leaped upon Will Stutely; but Stutely held his own sword in his hand beneath his robe, so he drew it forth before the constable came upon him. Then the constable struck a mighty blow; but Stutely, parrying the blow right deftly, smote the constable back again. Then he would have escaped, but that the constable, all dizzy with the wound, seized him by the knees as he reeled and fell. The others rushed upon him, and one smote him a blow upon the crown so that the blood ran down his face and blinded him. Then, staggering, he fell, and all sprang upon him, and bound him with hempen cords.

Now Robin Hood stood under the greenwood tree, thinking of Will Stutely and how he might be faring, when suddenly he saw running down the forest path the serving lass of the Blue Boar.

"Will Stutely hath been taken," cried she, "and I fear he is wounded sore. They have taken him to Nottingham Town, and I heard that he should be hanged tomorrow day."

"He shall not," cried Robin. "Or, if he be, full many a one shall have cause to cry alackaday!" Then he clapped his horn to his lips and blew three blasts, and presently sevenscore bold blades were gathered around him. "Now hark you all!" cried Robin. "Will Stutely hath been taken by that vile Sheriff's men, therefore doth it behoove us to take bow and brand in hand to bring him off again. Is it not so?" Then all cried "Aye!" with a great voice.

So the next day they wended their way from Sherwood Forest, but by different paths, in twos and threes, to meet in a tangled dell near to Nottingham Town. There Robin spoke thus: "Now we will lie here until we get news, for it doth behoove us to be wary."

They lay hidden until the sun stood high in the sky. The day was warm and the dusty road was bare of travelers, except an aged palmer. Robin called young David of Doncaster and said, "Now get thee forth and speak to yonder palmer, for he cometh from Nottingham Town, and may tell thee news of good Stutely."

So David strode forth and saluted the pilgrim and said, "Good morrow, holy father. Canst thou tell me when Will Stutely will be hanged upon the gallows tree? I fain would not miss the sight."

"Now, out upon thee, young man," cried the palmer, "that thou shouldst speak so when a good man is to be hanged!" And he struck his staff upon the ground in anger. "Even this day, toward evening, he shall be hanged, fourscore rods from the town gate of

Nottingham, where three roads meet; there the Sheriff sweareth he shall die as a warning to all outlaws. Alas! I say. Though Robin Hood and his band be outlaws, he taketh only from the rich and the dishonest." And the palmer went upon his way, muttering.

When David told Robin what the palmer had said, Robin called the band and spoke thus: "Now let us get to Nottingham Town and mix with the people there; but keep ye one another in sight, pressing near the prisoner and his guards when they come outside the walls. Strike no man without need, but if ye do strike, strike hard. Then keep together until we come again to Sherwood."

The sun was low in the western sky when a bugle note sounded from the castle wall. Then crowds filled the streets of Nottingham Town, for all knew that the famous Will Stutely was to be hanged. The castle gates opened wide and a great array of men-at-arms came forth with noise and clatter, the Sheriff riding at their head. In the midst of the guard, in a cart, with a halter about his neck, rode Will Stutely. His face was pale, and his fair hair was clotted where the blood had hardened. He looked up and he looked down, but though he saw some faces that showed pity and some that showed friendliness, he saw none that he knew.

At last they came to the great town gate, through which Stutely saw the fair country beyond. When he saw the slanting sunlight on field and fallow, on cot and farmhouse, and when he heard the birds singing their vespers, and the sheep bleating upon the hillside, there came a fullness to his heart so that salt tears blurred his sight, and he bowed his head lest the folk should think him unmanly. But when they were outside the walls he looked up again, and his heart leaped within him, for he saw upon all sides his own dear companions crowding closely upon the men-at-arms.

"Now, stand back!" cried the Sheriff in a mighty voice. "What mean ye, varlets, that ye push upon us so?"

Then came a bustle and a noise, and one strove to push between the men-at-arms, and Stutely saw that it was Little John.

"Now stand thou back!" cried one of the men-at-arms.

"Now stand thou back thine own self," quoth Little John, and smote the man a buffet beside his head that felled him as a butcher fells an ox, and then he leaped to the cart. With one stroke he cut the bonds that bound Stutely's arms and legs, and Stutely leaped straightway from the cart.

"Now as I live," cried the Sheriff, "yon varlet is a sturdy rebel! Take him, I bid you all, and let him not go!"

So saying, he spurred his horse upon Little John, and rising in his stirrups smote with might and main, but Little John ducked underneath the horse and the blow whistled over his head.

"Nay, good Sir Sheriff," cried he, leaping up again when the blow had passed, "I must e'en borrow thy sword." Thereupon he twitched the weapon deftly from out the Sheriff's hand. "Here, Stutely," he cried, "the Sheriff hath lent thee his sword! Back to back with me, man, and defend thyself, for help is nigh!"

Even as he spoke, a bugle horn sounded shrilly, and a cloth-yard shaft whistled within an inch of the Sheriff's head. Then came a swaying hither and thither, and oaths, cries and groans, and clashing of steel, and a score of arrows whistled through the air. And some cried, "Help!" and some, "A rescue, a rescue!"

"Treason!" bellowed the Sheriff. "Bear back! Bear back! Else we be all dead men!" Thereupon he reined his horse backward through the thickest of the crowd.

Now Robin Hood and his band might have slain half of the Sheriff's men had they desired to do so, but they let them push out of the press and get them gone.

"Oh, stay!" shouted Will Stutely after the Sheriff. "Thou wilt never catch bold Robin if thou dost not stand to meet him." But the Sheriff, bowing along his horse's back, only spurred the faster.

Then Will Stutely turned to Little John and wept aloud; and kissing his friend's cheeks, "Oh Little John!" quoth he. "Little did I reckon to see thy face this side of paradise."

Then Robin Hood gathered his band together in a close rank, with Will Stutely in the midst, and they moved slowly away toward Sherwood.

Thus the Sheriff of Nottingham tried thrice to take Robin Hood and failed each time; and the last time he was frightened for his life; so he said, "These men fear neither God nor man, nor king nor king's officers. I would sooner lose mine office than my life, so I will trouble them no more." So he kept close within his castle for many a day, and all the time he was gloomy and would speak to no one, for he was ashamed of what had happened that day.

Robin Hood Turns Butcher

NOW AFTER ALL THIS, Robin Hood said to himself, If I have the chance, I will make our worshipful Sheriff pay right well for that which he hath done to me. Maybe I may bring him to Sherwood to have a merry feast with us. For when Robin Hood caught a baron or a fat abbot or bishop, he brought him to the greenwood tree and feasted him before he lightened his purse.

But for nearly a year Robin Hood and his band lived quietly in Sherwood Forest, for Robin knew that it would not be wise for him to be seen in the neighborhood of Nottingham. At last he began to fret at his confinement; so one day he took up his cudgel and set forth to seek adventure. As he rambled along the sunlit road at the edge of Sherwood, he met a young butcher driving a fine mare and riding in a stout new cart, all hung about with meat. Merrily whistled the butcher as he jogged along.

"Good morrow to thee, jolly fellow," quoth Robin, "thou seemest happy this merry morn."

"And why should I not be so?" quoth the butcher. "Am I not hale in wind and limb? And am I not to be married to the bonniest lass in all Nottinghamshire on Thursday next?"

"Ha," said Robin, "and where goest thou with thy meat?"

"I go to the market at Nottingham Town," answered the butcher. "But who art thou, my fair friend?"

"A yeoman am I, and men do call me Robin Hood."

"Now, by Our Lady's grace," cried the butcher, "many a time have I heard thy deeds both sung and spoken of. But heaven forbid that thou shouldst take aught of me! An honest man am I."

"Not so much as one farthing would I take from thee, for I love a fair Saxon face—especially when the man that owneth it is to marry a bonny lass on Thursday next. But come"—and Robin Hood plucked the purse from his girdle—"here in this purse are six marks. Now, I would fain be a butcher for the day. Wilt thou take six marks for thy meat and thy horse and cart?"

"Now may the blessing of all the saints fall on thy head!" cried the butcher right joyfully, as he leaped down from his cart and took the purse that Robin held out to him.

"Now get thee gone back to thy lass, and give her a sweet kiss from me," quoth Robin, laughing. Then he donned the butcher's apron, climbed into the cart, took the reins and drove off.

When he came to Nottingham, he entered that part of the market where butchers stood, and opened his stall and spread his meat upon the bench. Then, taking his cleaver and steel and clattering them together, he sang:

> *"Lamb have I that hath fed upon naught*
> *But the dainty daisies pied,*
> *And the violet sweet, and the daffodil*
> *That grow fair streams beside.*
>
> *"And beef have I from the heathery wolds,*
> *And mutton from dales all green,*
> *And veal as white as a maiden's brow,*
> *With its mother's milk, I ween."*

Then he shouted lustily, "Now, who'll buy? Four prices have I. Three pennyworths of meat I sell to a fat friar or priest for sixpence, for I want not their custom; stout aldermen I charge threepence, for it doth not matter to me whether they buy or not; to buxom dames I sell three pennyworths for one penny, for I like their custom well; but to the bonny lass I charge naught but one fair kiss, for I like her custom the best of all."

Then all began to stare and wonder and to crowd around, and when they came to buy they found it as he had said, for he gave dames as much meat for one penny as they could buy elsewhere for three, and when a merry lass gave him a kiss, he charged not one penny for his meat; and many such came to his stall, for his eyes were as blue as the skies of June, and he gave to each full measure.

Thus he sold all his meat so fast that no butcher that stood near him could sell anything.

Then they began to talk among themselves, and some said, "This must be some thief who has stolen meat." But others said, "When did ye ever see a thief who parted with his goods so freely? This must be some prodigal who hath sold his father's land."

Then some of the butchers came to make his acquaintance. "Come, brother," quoth one, "we be all of one trade, so wilt thou go dine with us? For this day the Sheriff hath asked all the Butcher Guild to feast with him at the Guild Hall."

"Now, right joyously," quoth Robin, "will I go dine with you, my sweet lads, and that as fast as I can hie."

The Sheriff had already come in state to the Guild Hall, and with him many butchers. When Robin came in, those that were near the Sheriff whispered to him, "Yon is some prodigal that meaneth to spend his silver and gold right merrily."

Then the Sheriff called Robin, not knowing him in his butcher's dress, and made him sit on his right hand; for he loved a rich young prodigal—especially when he thought he might lighten that prodigal's pockets into his own most worshipful purse. So he made much of Robin. "Thou art a jolly blade," he said. "I love thee mightily." And he smote Robin upon the shoulder.

"Yea," quoth Robin. "I know thou dost love a jolly blade, for didst thou not have Robin Hood at thy shooting match and didst thou not give him a bright golden arrow for his own?"

At this the Sheriff laughed, but not as though he liked the jest. "Now thou art a merry soul," quoth he, "and I wot thou must have many a head of horned beasts and many an acre of land."

"Aye," quoth Robin, "five hundred and more horned beasts have I and my brothers, and none of them have we been able to sell, else I might not have turned butcher. As for my land, I have never asked my steward how many acres I have."

The Sheriff's eyes twinkled. "Nay, good youth," quoth he, "if thou canst not sell thy cattle, it may be I will lift them from thy hands myself. How much dost thou want for them?"

"Well," quoth Robin, "they are worth five hundred pounds."

"Nay," answered the Sheriff slowly. "Fain would I help thee, but I have not five hundred pounds. Yet I will give thee three hundred for them all."

"Now thou old miser!" quoth Robin. "Well thou knowest that so many cattle are worth seven hundred pounds, and yet I will take thine offer, for I and my brothers do need the money."

"I will bring thee the money," said the Sheriff. "But what is thy name, good youth?"

"Men call me Robert o' Locksley," quoth bold Robin.

"Then, good Robert o' Locksley," quoth the Sheriff, "I will come this day to see thy horned beasts."

"So be it," said Robin Hood, laughing, and smiting his palm upon the Sheriff's hand.

Thus the bargain was closed, but many of the butchers talked among themselves of the Sheriff, saying that it was but a scurvy trick to beguile a poor spendthrift youth in this way.

That afternoon the Sheriff and Robin Hood set forth, the Sheriff upon his horse and Robin running beside him, for he had sold his horse and cart to a trader. Thus they traveled till they came within the verge of Sherwood Forest. Then the Sheriff looked up and down and to the right and to the left. "Now," quoth he, "may heaven and its saints preserve us from that rogue Robin Hood."

"Nay," said Robin, laughing, "thou may'st set thy mind at rest, for well do I know Robin Hood and well do I know that thou art in no more danger from him this day than thou art from me."

At this the Sheriff looked askance at Robin, saying to himself, I like not that thou seemest so well acquainted with this outlaw.

But still they traveled deeper into the forest, and the deeper they went, the more quiet grew the Sheriff. At last they came to where the road took a sudden bend, and before them a herd of dun deer went tripping across the path. Then Robin came close to the Sheriff and, pointing his finger, he said, "These are my horned beasts, good Master Sheriff. Are they not fat and fair?"

At this the Sheriff drew rein quickly. "Now fellow," quoth he, "I would I were well out of this forest, for I like not thy company. Go thou thine own path, and let me but go mine."

But Robin caught the Sheriff's bridle rein. "Nay," cried he, "stay awhile, for I would thou shouldst see my brothers." So saying, he winded three notes upon his bugle and presently up the path came fivescore good stout yeomen with Little John at their head.

"What wouldst thou have, good master?" quoth Little John.

"Why," answered Robin, "dost thou not see our good master, the Sheriff, hath come to feast with us?"

Then all doffed their hats humbly, without smiling or seeming to be in jest, while Little John took the bridle rein and led the palfrey still deeper into the forest, all marching in order, with Robin Hood walking beside the Sheriff, hat in hand.

The Sheriff said never a word but his heart sank. So they came to the greenwood tree, and Robin sat down, placing the Sheriff at his right hand. "Now busk ye, my merry men," quoth he, "and bring forth meat and wine, for his worship feasted me in Nottingham Guild Hall today, and I would not have him go back empty."

Then, while bright fires crackled and savory smells of roasting venison filled the glade, did Robin Hood entertain the Sheriff right royally. First, couples stood forth at quarterstaff, and so quickly did they give stroke and parry that the Sheriff clapped his hands, forgetting where he was and crying aloud, "Well struck! Well struck!" Then all feasted together until the sun was low.

At last the Sheriff arose and said, "I thank you all, good yeomen, for the entertainment ye have given me. But I must away before darkness comes, lest I lose myself within the forest."

Then Robin said to the Sheriff, "If thou must go, worshipful sir, go thou must; but thou hast forgot something. We keep a merry inn here, but our guests must pay their reckoning."

The Sheriff laughed, but the laugh was hollow. "Well, jolly boys," quoth he, "we have had a merry time, and even if ye had not asked me, I would have given you a score of pounds."

"Nay," quoth Robin, "it would ill beseem us to treat your worship so meanly. By my faith, I would be ashamed to show my face if I did not reckon the King's deputy at three hundred pounds."

"Think ye that your beggarly feast was worth three pounds," roared the Sheriff, "let alone three hundred?"

"Speak not so roundly, your worship," quoth Robin gravely, "for there be those here who love thee not so much. Look down the cloth and thou wilt see Will Stutely. Now pay thy score without more ado, or it may fare ill with thee."

As he spoke the Sheriff's ruddy cheeks grew pale, and slowly he drew forth his purse.

"Now, Little John," quoth Robin, "see that the reckoning be right. We would not doubt our Sheriff, but he might not like it if he should find he had not paid his full score."

Little John counted the money and found that the bag held three hundred pounds in silver and gold. But to the Sheriff it seemed as if every clink of the bright money was a drop of blood from his veins. And when he saw it all counted out in a heap, he turned away and silently mounted his horse. Then Robin, taking the bridle rein, led him into the main forest path. "Fare thee well," he said, "and when next thou thinkest to despoil some poor prodigal, remember thy feast in Sherwood Forest." He clapped his hand to the horse's back, and off went nag and Sheriff.

Then bitterly the Sheriff rued the day that first he meddled with Robin Hood, for all men laughed at him and many ballads were sung of how the Sheriff went to shear and came home shorn.

How Robin Hood Found New Recruits

ONE FINE DAY, ROBIN HOOD and two chosen fellows of his band, Little John and Arthur a Bland, were traveling along a sunny road when Robin waxed thirsty; so, there being a fountain of water just behind the hedgerow, they crossed a stile and came to where the water bubbled up from beneath a mossy stone. Kneeling and making cups of the palms of their hands, they drank their fill, and then, the spot being shady, they stretched their limbs and rested.

"Heyday!" quoth Robin, who had been gazing around him. "Yon is a gaily feathered bird."

The others looked and saw a young man walking slowly down the highway. His doublet was of scarlet silk and his stockings also;

a handsome sword hung by his side, the embossed leathern scabbard being picked out with fine threads of gold; his cap was of scarlet velvet, and a broad feather hung down behind one ear. His hair was long and yellow and curled upon his shoulders.

"Truly, his clothes have overmuch prettiness," quoth Arthur, "but his shoulders are broad and his arms dangle not down like spindles, but hang stiff and bend at the elbow. I take my vow, there be no bread-and-milk limbs in those fine clothes."

"Pah!" quoth Robin Hood. "I take it thou art wrong. Were a furious mouse to run across his path, he would cry, 'La!' and fall straightway into a swoon. I wonder who he may be."

"Some great baron's son, I doubt not," answered Little John, "with good and true men's money lining his purse."

"Aye, marry, that is true, I make no doubt," quoth Robin. "What a pity that such men should have good fellows, whose shoes they are not fit to tie, dancing at their bidding. Now, lie ye both here, while I show you how I drub this fellow." So saying, Robin Hood crossed the stile and stood in the road, with his hands on his hips, in the stranger's path.

Meantime the stranger neither quickened his pace nor seemed to see that such a man as Robin Hood was in the world.

"Hold!" cried Robin, when the other had come close to him. "Hold! Stand where thou art!"

"Wherefore should I hold, good fellow?" said the stranger in a gentle voice. "Ne'ertheless, as thou dost desire that I should stay, I will abide for a short time."

"Then," quoth Robin, "I would have thee deliver to me thy purse, fair friend, that I may look into it, and judge whether thou hast more wealth about thee than our law allows."

"Alas," said the youth with a smile, "I do love to hear thee talk, thou pretty fellow, but I have nothing to give thee. Let me go my way, I prithee."

"Nay, thou goest not," quoth Robin, "till thou hast shown me thy purse." So saying, he raised his quarterstaff above his head.

"Alas!" said the stranger sadly. "I fear much that I must slay thee, thou poor fellow!" So saying, he drew his sword.

25

"Put by thy weapon," quoth Robin. "It cannot stand against my staff. Yonder is a good oaken thicket; take a cudgel thence and defend thyself fairly."

Then the stranger stepped to the little clump of ground oaks Robin had spoken of. Presently he found a sapling to his liking. Rolling up his sleeves, he laid hold of it, placed his heel against the ground and, with one mighty pull, plucked the young tree up by the roots. Then he came back, trimming away the roots and stems with his sword as quietly as if he had done naught to speak of.

When Little John and Arthur saw the stranger drag the sapling up from the earth, and heard the rending and snapping of its roots, Arthur pursed his lips together, drawing his breath between them in a long inward whistle.

"By the breath of my body!" said Little John. "I think our poor master will stand but an ill chance with yon fellow."

Whatever Robin Hood thought, he stood his ground, and now he and the stranger stood face to face. Back and forth they fought, the dust of the highway rising about them like a cloud. Thrice Robin struck the stranger, but at last the stranger struck Robin's cudgel so fairly in the middle that he not only beat down Robin's guard, but gave him such a rap that down he tumbled in the road.

"Hold!" cried Robin Hood, when he saw the stranger raising his staff once more. "I yield me!"

"Alas!" cried Little John, bursting from his cover, with a twinkle in his eye. "Thou art in an ill plight, good master. Thy jerkin is all befouled with the dust of the road. Let me help thee to arise."

"A plague on thy aid!" cried Robin angrily. "I can get to my feet without thy help." Then, turning to the stranger, he said, "What may be thy name, good fellow?"

"My name is Gamwell," answered the other.

"Ha!" cried Robin. "Is it even so? I have near kin of that name. Whence camest thou, fair friend?"

"From Maxfield Town I come," answered the stranger, "to seek my mother's young brother, whom men call Robin Hood."

"Will Gamwell!" cried Robin, placing both hands upon the other's shoulders. "Dost thou not know me, lad?"

26

"Now, by the breath of my body!" cried the other. "I do believe that thou art mine own Uncle Robin." And each flung his arms around the other, kissing him upon the cheek.

"Why, how now," quoth Robin, "what change is here? Verily, some ten years ago I left thee a stripling lad, with great joints and ill-hung limbs, and lo! Here thou art, as tight a fellow as e'er I set mine eyes upon. Dost thou remember, lad, how I showed thee the proper way to throw out thy bow arm?"

"Yea," said young Gamwell, "and I thought thee so above all other men that, I make my vow, had I known who thou wert, I would never have dared to lift hand against thee this day. I trust I did thee no great harm."

"No, no, thou didst not harm me," quoth Robin hastily. "Yet thou art the strongest man that ever I laid eyes upon. But tell me, how camest thou to leave Sir Edward and thy mother?"

"Alas!" answered young Gamwell. "It is an ill story, Uncle. My father's steward was a saucy varlet, and I know not why my father kept him, saving that he did oversee with great judgment, and that my father was ever slow to anger. Well, one day that saucy fellow sought to berate my father, I standing by. I could stand it no longer, good Uncle, so I gave him a box o' the ear, and—wouldst thou believe it?—the fellow straightway died o't. I think they said I broke his neck. So off they packed me to seek thee and escape the law."

"Well, by my faith," quoth Robin, "for anyone escaping the law, thou wert taking it the most easily that ever I beheld."

"Nay, Uncle," answered Will Gamwell, "overhaste never churned good butter. Moreover, I do verily believe that this over-strength of my body hath taken the nimbleness out of my heels."

"In truth," quoth Robin, "I am glad to see thee, Will. But thou must change thy name, for warrants will be out against thee; so, because of thy clothes, thou shalt be called Will Scarlet."

"Will Scarlet," quoth Little John, stepping forward and reaching out his great palm, which the other took, "the name fitteth thee well. Thou art like to achieve fame, Will, for there will be many a merry ballad sung about the country of how Robin Hood bit off so large a piece of cake that he choked on it."

"Nay, good Little John, let us keep this day's doing among ourselves," cried Robin, biting his nether lip, while the others could not forbear laughing. "Come, we will return to Sherwood."

So, turning their backs, they retraced their steps. Now, when the four had traveled for a long time, "How now!" quoth Robin suddenly. "Who may yon fellow be coming along the road?"

"Truly," said Little John, "I think he is a certain young miller I have seen now and then around the edge of Sherwood."

As the young miller came near they could see that his clothes were dusted with flour, and over his back he carried a great sack of meal, and across the sack was a thick quarterstaff. His limbs were stout and strong, and his cheeks ruddy as a winter hip; his hair was flaxen, and on his chin was a downy growth of beard.

"Now let us have a merry jest with this good fellow," quoth Robin Hood. "We will pretend to rob him of his honest gains. Then will we give him a feast in the forest and send him home with crowns in his purse for every penny he hath." Whereupon all four of them ran out and surrounded the miller.

"Hold, friend!" cried Robin. "We be good Christian men and would fain help thee by carrying part of thy heavy load."

"I give you all thanks," said the miller, "but my bag is none that heavy that I cannot carry it e'en by myself."

"Nay, thou dost mistake," quoth Robin. "I meant that thou mightest have some heavy farthings or pence about thee, not to speak of silver."

"Alas!" cried the miller, throwing the great sack to the ground. "I have not about me so much as a groat. Let me depart in peace, I pray you. Moreover, let me tell you that ye are upon Robin Hood's ground, and should he find you seeking to rob an honest craftsman, he will clip your ears to your heads."

"In truth I fear Robin Hood no more than I do myself," quoth jolly Robin. "Good Arthur, empty that fat sack upon the ground; I warrant thou wilt find a shilling or two in the flour."

"Spoil not my good meal!" cried the miller, falling upon his knees. "Spare it, and I will give up the money in the bag."

Slowly and unwillingly the miller untied the mouth of the bag, and slowly thrust his hands into the flour. The others gathered around him, looking and wondering what he would bring forth. But while he pretended to be searching for the money, the miller gathered two great handfuls of meal. "Ha," quoth he, "here they are, the beauties." As the others leaned still more forward to see what he had, he suddenly cast the meal into their faces, filling their eyes and noses and mouths with the flour. Then, while all four stumbled about, roaring with the smart of it, and rubbed their eyes till the tears made great channels on their faces through the meal, the miller threw another handful of flour and another and another, till their hair and beards and clothes were white as snow.

Then, catching up his great staff, the miller began laying about him as though he were clean gone mad. This way and that skipped the four, like peas on a drumhead, but they could see neither to defend themselves nor to run away. Thwack! Thwack! went the miller's cudgel across their backs, and at every blow great white clouds of flour rose in the air and went drifting down the breeze.

"Stop!" roared Robin at last. "Give over! I am Robin Hood!"

"Thou liest, knave," cried the miller. "Stout Robin never robbed an honest tradesman." And he gave him another blow. "Nay, thou art not getting thy share, thou long-legged knave." And he smote Little John so that he sent him skipping half across the road. "It is thy turn now, black beard." And he gave Arthur a crack. "How now, red coat, let me brush the dust from thee!" cried he, smiting Will Scarlet. And so he gave them merry words and blows until at last Robin found his horn and blew three blasts upon it.

Now it chanced that Will Stutely and a party of men were in the glade not far away. So they dashed forward with might and main and burst from the covert into the highroad. But what a sight they saw! Five men stood there white with meal from top to toe, for much of the flour had fallen back upon the miller.

"What is thy need, master?" cried Will Stutely. "And what doth all this mean?"

Hereupon, while he and the others rubbed the meal from their eyes and brushed their clothes clean, Robin told them all.

"Quick, men, seize the vile miller!" cried Stutely, who was nigh choking with laughter. Whereupon several seized the stout fellow, and bound his arms behind his back with bowstrings.

"Ha!" cried Robin, when they brought the miller to him. "Thou wouldst murder me, wouldst thou? By my faith—" Here he stopped and stood glaring upon the miller grimly. But Robin's anger could not hold, so in spite of all he broke into a laugh. And when they saw their master laugh, the yeomen could contain themselves no longer, and a mighty shout of laughter went up.

"What is thy name, good fellow?" said Robin.

"Alas, sir, I am Midge, the Miller's son," said the miller.

"I make my vow," quoth Robin, "thou art the mightiest Midge that e'er I beheld. Now wilt thou leave thy dusty mill and join my band? By my faith, thou art too stout a man to spend thy days betwixt the hopper and the till."

"Then truly, if thou dost forgive me for the blows I struck, I will join with thee right merrily," said the miller.

"Then have I gained this day," quoth Robin, "the two stoutest yeomen in all Nottinghamshire. We will get us away to the greenwood tree, and there hold a feast in honor of our new friends." So saying, he turned and led the way into the forest.

Robin Hood and Allan a Dale

Two DAYS HAD PASSED BY, yet still, when Robin moved of a sudden, pain here and there would, as it were, jog him, crying, "Thou hast had a drubbing, good fellow." The day was bright and jocund, and he sat under the greenwood tree; on one side was Will Scarlet, lying upon his back, gazing up into the clear sky, with hands clasped behind his head; upon the other side sat Little John, fashioning a cudgel out of a stout crab-tree limb. Elsewhere upon the grass sat many others of the band.

"By my faith," quoth Robin, "our money groweth low in the purse, for no one hath come to pay a reckoning for many a day. Now choose thee six men, good Stutely, and get thee to Fosse Way, and bring rich guests to eat with us this evening."

"Truly, my limbs do grow slack through abiding idly here," quoth Stutely, springing to his feet. "As for two of my six, I will choose Midge the Miller and Will Scarlet, for, as well thou knowest, good master, they are stout fists at the quarterstaff."

At this all laughed but Robin, who twisted up his face. "I can speak for them," said he.

So, having chosen four more stout fellows, Will Stutely and his band set forth. For all the livelong day they abided near Fosse Way, but no guest such as they desired showed his face. At last the sun began to sink. Then Stutely arose. "A plague of such ill luck!" quoth he. "Come, lads, let us pack up and home again, say I."

Accordingly, the others arose, and they all turned back to Sherwood. After they had gone some distance, Will Stutely suddenly stopped. "Hist!" quoth he. "Methinks I hear a sound." At this all stopped and listened with bated breath; and they heard a faint and melancholy sound, like someone in lamentation.

"Ha!" quoth Will Scarlet. "This must be looked into." Thus saying, he led the way to an opening in the woodland, whence a brook spread out into a glassy-pebbled pool. By the side of this pool, and beneath a willow, lay a youth, weeping aloud. From the branches overhead hung a beautiful harp inlaid with gold and silver. Beside him lay a stout ashen bow and half a score of arrows.

"Halloa!" shouted Will Stutely. "Who art thou, fellow, that liest there killing the green grass with salt water?"

Hearing the voice, the stranger sprang to his feet and, snatching up his bow and fitting a shaft, held himself in readiness for whatever ill might befall him.

"Pah!" cried Will Stutely. "Wipe thine eyes, man! I hate to see a tall, stout fellow sniveling like a girl of fourteen over a dead tomtit. Put down thy bow! We mean thee no harm."

But Will Scarlet, seeing how the young stranger was stung by Stutely's words, came up to him and put his hand upon his shoulder. "Nay, thou art in trouble, poor boy!" said he kindly. "Mind not these fellows. They are rough, but they mean thee well. Thou shalt come with us, and perchance we may find a certain one that can aid thee in thy perplexities."

"Yea, truly," said Will Stutely gruffly, "I meant no harm. Take down thy singing tool, and away with us."

With bowed head and sorrowful steps, the youth did as he was bidden. A glimmering gray fell over all things, and the strange whispering sounds of nighttime came to the ear. At last they came to the open glade, now bathed in pale moonlight. In the center crackled a great fire, throwing a red glow all around; and the air was filled with the sweet smell of good things cooking.

So, with Will Scarlet upon one side and Stutely upon the other, the stranger came to where Robin sat under the greenwood tree.

"Good even, fair friend," said Robin. "And hast thou come to feast with me this day?"

"Alas! I know not," said the lad, looking around him with dazed eyes. "Truly, I know not whether I be in a dream."

"Nay, marry," quoth Robin, laughing, "thou art awake, as thou wilt presently find, for a fine feast is a-cooking for thee."

Still the stranger looked about him. "Methinks," said he at last, "I know now where I am. Art not thou the great Robin Hood?"

"Thou hast hit the bull's-eye," quoth Robin, clapping him upon the shoulder. "Sin' thou knowest me, thou knowest also that he who feasteth with me must pay his reckoning."

"Alas!" said the stranger. "I have no money, saving only the half of a sixpence, the other half of which mine own dear love doth carry, hung about her neck by a silken thread."

At this Robin turned sharply to Will Stutely. "How now," quoth he, "is this the guest thou hast brought to fill our purse?"

Up spoke Will Scarlet, and told how they had found the lad in sorrow, and how they had brought him to Robin, thinking that he might aid him. Then Robin Hood placed his hand upon the youth's shoulder and held him off at arm's length, scanning his face.

"A young face," quoth he in a low voice, "a fair face. But, if I may judge, grief cometh to young as well as to old." At these words, spoken so kindly, the lad's eyes brimmed up with tears. "Nay," said Robin hastily, "cheer up, lad. I warrant thy case is not so bad that it cannot be mended. What may be thy name?"

"Allan a Dale is my name, good master."

"Allan a Dale," repeated Robin, musing. "Surely thou art the minstrel of whom we have been hearing lately, whose voice so charmeth all men. Dost thou not come from Rotherstream?"

"Yea, truly," answered Allan, "I do come thence."

"How old art thou, Allan?" said Robin.

"I am but twenty years of age."

"Methinks thou art overyoung to be perplexed with trouble," quoth Robin kindly. Then, turning to the others, he cried, "Come, lads, busk ye and get our feast; only thou, Will Scarlet, and thou, Little John, stay here." Then Robin turned once more to the youth. "Now, lad," said he, "sit thou beside me, and tell us thy troubles. A flow of words doth ever ease the heart of sorrows."

Then the youth told all that was in his heart; at first in broken words and phrases, then freely when he saw that all listened closely to what he said. He told them how he had come from York to the vale of Rother, traveling the country through as a minstrel, stopping now at castle, now at hall; and how one evening in a certain farmhouse he sang before a stout franklin and a maiden as pure and lovely as the first snowdrop of spring; and how sweet Ellen had listened to him and had loved him. He told how he had watched for her when she went abroad, but was all too afraid to speak to her, until at last, beside the banks of Rother, he had spoken of his love, and she had whispered that which had made his heartstrings quiver for joy. Then they broke a sixpence between them, and vowed to be true to one another forever.

Next he told how her father had discovered what was a-doing, and had taken her away from him; how this morn, only one short month and a half from the time that he had seen her last, he had heard that she was to marry old Sir Stephen of Trent two days hence, for Ellen's father thought it would be a grand thing to have his daughter marry so high, albeit she wished it not.

"By the breath of my body," burst forth Little John. "I have a mind to go straightway and cudgel the nasty life out of that same vile Sir Stephen. Does an old weazen think that tender lasses are to be bought like pullets o' a market day?"

Then up spoke Will Scarlet. "Methinks it seemeth but ill done of the lass that she should so quickly change at others' bidding. I like it not in her, Allan."

"Nay," said Allan hotly, "thou dost wrong her. She is as gentle as a stockdove. She may do her father's bidding, but if she marries Sir Stephen, her heart will break and she will die."

While the others were speaking, Robin had been sunk in thought. "I have a plan might fit thy case, Allan," said he. "If thy true love's father be the man I take him to be, he shall give you both his blessing as wedded man and wife, in the place of old Sir Stephen and upon his wedding morn. But stay, there's one thing reckoned not upon—the priest. Those of the cloth do not love me overmuch, and in such a matter they are like to prove stiff-necked."

"So far as that goeth," quoth Will Scarlet, "I know of a certain friar that would do thy business, couldst thou but get on the soft side of him. He is known as the Curtal Friar of Fountain Dale. A stout pair of legs could carry a man to his cell and back in a day."

"Then give me thy hand, Allan," cried Robin, "and I swear by the bright hair of Saint Ælfrida that this time two days hence Ellen a Dale shall be thy wife."

But now one came to say that the feast was ready; so, Robin leading the way, the others followed to where the meal was spread upon the grass. When they had eaten, Robin Hood turned to Allan. "Now, Allan," quoth he, "so much has been said of thy singing that we would fain have a taste of thy skill ourselves."

"Surely!" answered Allan readily, and, taking up his harp, he ran his fingers lightly over the strings. Then, backing his voice with music on his harp, he sang many a sweet ballad.

Not a sound broke the stillness while Allan a Dale sang; so sweet was his voice that each man sat with bated breath.

"By my faith and my troth," quoth Robin when at last the minstrel had done, "thou must not leave our company, Allan! Wilt thou not stay with us here in the forest?"

Then Allan took Robin's hand and kissed it. "I will stay with thee always, dear master," said he, "for never have I known such kindness as thou hast shown me this day."

And thus Allan a Dale became one of Robin Hood's band.

34

THE YEOMEN OF SHERWOOD were ever early risers of a morn, more especially when the summertime had come, for then the dew was the brightest, and the song of the birds the sweetest.

Quoth Robin, "Now will I go to seek this same Friar of Fountain Dale of whom we spoke yesternight, and I will take with me Little John, Will Scarlet, David of Doncaster and Arthur a Bland. Bide the rest of you here, and Will Stutely shall be your chief while I am gone." Then straightway Robin Hood donned a fine steel coat of chain mail, over which he put on a light jacket of Lincoln green. His head he covered with a cap of soft white leather, in which stood a nodding cock's plume. By his side he hung a good broadsword of bluish tempered steel. A gallant sight was Robin so arrayed, the glint of steel showing here and there as the sunlight caught the links of polished mail that showed beneath his green coat.

So he and the four yeomen set forth, Will Scarlet taking the lead, for he knew whither to go. Thus they strode mile after mile, now along a sunlit road, now adown some sweet forest path, till at last they came to a wide, glassy and lily-padded stream. Here a path stretched along the banks, on which labored the horses that tugged slow-moving barges, laden with barley meal, from the countryside to the town. But now, in the hot silence of the midday no horse was seen nor any man besides themselves.

"Now, good Uncle," quoth Will Scarlet, "just beyond yon bend is a ford no deeper than thy mid-thigh, and on the other side is the friar's little hermitage."

"Had I thought I should have to wade water," quoth Robin, "I had donned other clothes. But no matter, now, for a wetting will not wash the skin away. But bide ye here, lads, for I would enjoy this merry adventure alone." So saying, he strode onward.

Now Robin had walked no farther than where the bend of the path hid his men from his view when he stopped suddenly, for he thought that he heard voices. The sound came from over behind the bank, that here dropped steep a half a score of feet to the verge of the river. Robin laid him softly down upon the grass and peered over the edge.

All was cool and shady beneath the bank. A stout willow leaned across the water. All around grew feathery ferns, and up to Robin's nostrils came the tender odor of the wild thyme that loves the moist verges of streams. Here, with his back against the trunk of the tree, sat a brawny fellow, but no other man was there. His head was as round as a ball, and covered with a mat of close-clipped, curly black hair that grew low on his forehead. But his crown was shorn as smooth as the palm of one's hand, which, together with his loose robe, cowl, and string of beads, showed that which his looks never would have done, that he was a friar. His cheeks were nearly covered with a curly black beard, and his shoulders were e'en a match for those of Little John himself. Beneath his black brows danced a pair of little gray eyes that could not stand still for very drollery of humor. By his side lay a steel cap, and betwixt his knees he held a great pasty. In his right fist he held a piece of brown crust at which he munched sturdily, and every now and then he thrust his left hand into the pie and drew it forth full of meat.

The friar, all unknowing that he was overlooked, ate his meal placidly. At last he was done, and, having first wiped his hands upon the thyme (and sweeter napkin ne'er had king in all the world), he took up a flask that lay beside him and began talking to, and answering, himself as though he were another man.

"Dear lad, thou art the sweetest fellow; I do love thee as a lover loveth his lass. La, thou dost make me shamed to speak so to me in this solitary place, and yet if thou wilt have me say so, I do love thee as thou lovest me. Nay then, wilt thou not take a drink of good malmsey? After thee, lad, after thee. Nay, I beseech thee, sweeten the draught with thy lips. [Here he took a long, deep draught.] And now, sweet lad, 'tis thy turn. [Here he passed the bottle from his left hand to his right.] I take it, and here's wishing thee as much good as thou wishest me." Saying this, he took another draught, and truly he drank enough for two.

36

All this time Robin listened, while his stomach so quaked with laughter that he was forced to press his palm across his mouth to keep it from bursting forth; for, truly, he would not have spoiled such a goodly jest for the half of Nottinghamshire.

Having gotten his breath from his last draught, the friar began talking again in this wise: "Now, sweet lad, canst thou not sing me a song? La, I am in but ill voice this day; dost thou not hear how I croak like a frog? Nay, nay, thy voice is as sweet as any bullfinch. Come, methinks that thou and I might sing together; dost thou not know a dainty little catch called 'The Loving Youth and the Scornful Maid'? Methinks that thou couldst take the lass's part if I take the lad's? I know not but I will try."

Then, singing first with a voice deep and gruff, and anon in one high and squeaking, he blithely trolled the merry catch of "The Loving Youth and The Scornful Maid":

"HE: *Ah, it's wilt thou come with me, my love?*
And it's wilt thou, love, be mine?
For I will give unto thee, my love,
   Gay knots and ribbons so fine.
I'll woo thee, love, on my bended knee,
And I'll pipe sweet songs to none but thee.
      Then it's hark! hark! hark!
      To the winged lark,
   And it's hark to the cooing dove!
      And the bright daffodil
      Groweth down by the rill,
   So come thou and be my love.

"SHE: *Now get thee away, young man so fine;*
   Now get thee away, I say;
For my true love shall never be thine,
   And so thou hadst better not stay.
Thou art not a fine enough lad for me,
So I'll wait till a better young man I see."

Here Robin could contain himself no longer but burst forth into a mighty roar of laughter; then, as the friar did not seem to have heard him but kept on with the song, he joined in the chorus, and together they sang, or as one might say, bellowed:

> *"For it's hark! hark! hark!*
> *To the joyous lark,*
> *And it's hark to the cooing dove!*
> *For the bright daffodil*
> *Groweth down by the rill,*
> *Yet never I'll be thy love."*

But no sooner had the last word been sung than the holy man clapped his steel cap on his head, and springing to his feet cried in a great voice, "What spy have we here? Come forth, thou limb of evil, and I will carve thee into as fine pudding meat as e'er a wife cooked of a Sunday." Hereupon he drew from beneath his robe a great broadsword full as stout as Robin's.

"Nay, put up thy pinking iron, friend," quoth Robin. "Folk who have sung so sweetly together should not fight thereafter." Hereupon he leaped down the bank. "I tell thee, friend," said he, "my throat is as parched with that song as e'er a barley stubble in October. Hast thou haply any malmsey left?"

"Truly," said the friar, "thou dost ask thyself freely where thou art not bidden. Yet I am too good a Christian to refuse any man drink that is athirst." And he held the bottle out to Robin.

Putting it to his lips, Robin tilted his head back, while that which was within said *glug! glug! glug!* for more than three winks, I wot. When Robin was done, the friar took the bottle quickly. He shook it, looked reproachfully at the yeoman, and straightway placed it at his own lips. When it came away again there was naught within it.

Then said Robin, laughing, "Dost thou know of one hereabout who goeth by the name of Curtal Friar of Fountain Dale?"

"Yea, somewhat," answered the other dryly.

"I do wish," quoth Robin, looking thoughtfully at the priest, "to cross yon ford and find this friar. But I fain would not get my fine clothes wet. Methinks thy shoulders are stout and broad. Couldst thou not find it in thy heart to carry me across?"

"Now, by the white hand of the holy Lady of the Fountain!" burst forth the friar in a mighty rage. "Dost thou, thou poor puny stripling, ask me, the holy Tuck, to carry thee? Now I swear—" Here he paused suddenly, then the anger passed from his face, and his little eyes twinkled once more. "But why should I not?" quoth he piously. "Did not the holy Saint Christopher ever carry the stranger across the river? And should I, poor sinner that I am, be ashamed to do likewise? Come with me, stranger, and I will do thy bidding in an humble frame of mind." So saying, he led the way to the shallow pebbly ford.

Having come to the ford, he girded up his robes about his loins, tucked his good broadsword beneath his arm and stooped his back to take Robin upon it. Suddenly he straightened up. "Methinks," quoth he, "thou'lt get thy weapon wet. Let me tuck it beneath mine arm along with mine own, for I would carry it as a penance to my pride."

So Robin handed his sword to the other. Then once more the friar bent his back and, Robin having mounted, he stepped into the water and so strode onward, splashing in the shoal and breaking the surface into ever widening rings. At last he reached the other side and Robin leaped lightly from his back.

"Many thanks, good father," quoth he. "Prithee, now, give me my sword and let me away, for I am in haste."

At this the stout friar looked upon Robin, with head on one side, and slowly winked his right eye. "Nay, good youth," said he. "I doubt not that thou art in haste with thine affairs, yet thou dost think nothing of mine. Thine are of a carnal nature; mine are of a spiritual nature. Moreover, mine affairs do lie upon the other side of this stream. I see by thy quest of this holy recluse that thou art a good man. I did get wet coming hither, and am sadly afraid that should I wade the water again I might get certain cricks i' the joints that would mar my devotions for many a day to come. I know that since I have so humbly done thy bidding thou wilt carry me back again. Thou see'st how Saint Godrick, that holy hermit whose natal day this is, hath placed in my hands two swords and in thine never a one."

"Thou cunning friar," quoth Robin, biting his lips, "thou hast me fair enow. I might have known from thy looks that thou wert no such holy man as thou didst pretend to be. Yet give me my sword and I do promise to carry thee back straightway. I will not lift the weapon against thee."

"Marry," quoth the friar, "I fear thee not. Here is thy skewer; and get thyself ready, for I would hasten back."

So Robin took his sword again and buckled it at his side; then he bent his stout back and took the friar upon it.

Now I wot Robin Hood had a heavier load to carry in the friar than the friar had in him. Moreover he did not know the ford, so he went stumbling among the stones while the sweat ran down his face in beads. Meantime, the friar dug his heels into Robin's sides and bade him hasten, calling him many ill names the while. To all this Robin answered never a word, but softly felt around till he found the buckle of the belt that held the friar's sword. So, when Robin stood on dry land and the friar leaped from his back, the yeoman gripped hold of the friar's sword so that it came away from the holy man.

"Now," quoth Robin, panting, "I have thee, fellow. This time that saint of whom thou didst speak hath delivered two swords into my hand. If thou dost not carry me back, and speedily, I will prick thy skin till it is as full of holes as a slashed doublet."

The friar looked at Robin with a grim look. "I knew not that thou wert so cunning," said he. "Truly, thou hast me upon the hip. Give me my sword, and I promise not to draw it save in self-defense; also, I promise to take thee upon my back."

So Robin gave him his sword, which the friar buckled to his side more securely; then tucking up his robes once more, he took Robin upon his back and stepped into the water, while Robin sat there laughing. At last he reached the middle, where the water was deepest. Here he stopped and, with a sudden heave of his shoulders, shot Robin over his head as though he were a sack of grain.

Down went Robin into the water with a mighty splash. "There," quoth the holy man, calmly turning back again to the shore, "let that cool thy hot spirit, if it may."

Robin got to his feet, the water running from him in little rills. He shot the water out of his ears and spat some out of his mouth, and, gathering his scattered wits, saw the stout friar laughing on the bank. "Stay, thou villain!" roared Robin. "I am after thee straight, and if I do not carve thy brawn for thee, may I never lift finger again!" So saying, he dashed, splashing, to the bank.

"Thou needst not hasten," quoth the friar. "I will abide here."

And now Robin began to roll up his sleeves. The friar, also, tucked his robes more about him, showing a great, stout arm on which the muscles stood out like humps of an aged tree. Then Robin saw that the friar had also a coat of chain mail beneath his gown.

"Look to thyself," cried Robin, drawing his good sword.

"Aye, marry," quoth the friar, who held his already in his hand. And thereupon began a mighty battle. The swords flashed in the sun and then met with a clash that sounded far and near. For an hour or more they strove, yet neither harmed the other.

At last Robin cried, "Hold thy hand, good friend! I crave a boon of thee, ere we begin again." For he began to think that it would be an ill thing either to be smitten or to smite so stout a fellow.

"What wouldst thou have of me?" asked the friar.

"Only that thou wilt let me blow upon my horn."

The friar bent his brows. "Now I do think that thou hast some cunning trick in this," quoth he. "Ne'ertheless, I will let thee have thy wish, providing thou wilt let me blow upon my whistle."

"With all my heart," quoth Robin. So saying, he raised his silver horn to his lips and blew thrice upon it, clear and high.

Scarcely had the echo of the last note of Robin's bugle come winding back from across the river when four tall men in Lincoln green came running around the bend of the path, each with a bow in his hand and an arrow ready nocked upon the string.

"Ha! Is it thus, thou traitor knave!" cried the friar. "Then, marry, look to thyself!" So saying, he clapped a little silver whistle to his lips and blew a shrill blast. And now there came a crackling of the bushes that lined the path, and forth from the covert burst four great, shaggy hounds. "At 'em," cried the friar, pointing to where the yeomen were standing stock-still with wonder.

As the hawk darts upon its quarry, so sped the dogs at the yeo-men; and it would have been an ill day had not Will Scarlet stepped forth and met the dogs as they came rushing. "How now, Fangs!" cried he sternly. "Down, Beauty! What means this?"

At the sound of his voice each dog came to him straightway and licked his hands, as is the wont of dogs that meet one they know. "Why, how now!" cried the stout friar. "Art thou a wizard to turn those wolves into lambs? Ha! Can I trust mine eyes? What means it that I see young Master Gamwell in such company?"

"Nay, Tuck," said the young man, as the four came forward, "my name is no longer Will Gamwell, but Will Scarlet; and this is my good uncle, Robin Hood."

"Truly, good master," said the friar, reaching out his great palm to Robin, "I ha' oft heard thy name. I crave thy forgiveness, and wonder not that I found so stout a man against me. But, Master Will, how is it that thou dost abide in Sherwood?"

"Why, Tuck, dost thou not know of my ill happening with my father's steward?" answered Scarlet.

"Yea, truly, yet I knew not that thou wert in hiding because of it. Marry, the times are all awry when a gentleman must lie hidden for so small a thing."

"But we are losing time," quoth Robin, "and I have yet to find the Curtal Friar of Fountain Dale."

"Why, Uncle," said Will Scarlet, "he stands beside thee."

"How?" quoth Robin to the friar. "Art thou the man I have been at such pains to seek all day, and have got such a ducking for?"

"Why, truly," said the friar demurely, "some do call me the Curtal Friar of Fountain Dale; others call me simply Friar Tuck."

"I like the last name best," quoth Robin, "for it doth slip more glibly off the tongue. But why didst thou not tell me?"

"Why, truly, thou didst not ask me, good master," quoth stout Tuck. "But what didst thou desire of me?"

"Nay," quoth Robin, "the day groweth late. Come back with us to Sherwood, and I will unfold all to thee as we travel."

So they all departed, with the dogs at their heels; but it was long past nightfall ere they reached the greenwood tree.

AND NOW HAD COME the morning when fair Ellen was to be married, and on which Robin Hood had sworn that Allan a Dale should, as it were, eat out of the platter that had been filled for Sir Stephen of Trent. Up rose Robin, blithe and gay, up rose his merry men, and up rose last of all Friar Tuck, winking the smart of sleep from out his eyes.

"Now," quoth Robin, when they had broken their fast, "it is time to set forth upon the undertaking that we have in hand. I will choose one score of my good men to go with me; thou, Will Scarlet, wilt be the chief here while I am gone." Then Robin called Little John and Will Stutely and other famous lads of whom I have told you. And after the score were chosen, Robin donned a gay, beribboned coat such as might have been worn by some minstrel, and slung a harp across his shoulder; and the band stared and laughed, for never had they seen their master in such a fantastic guise before.

"Truly," quoth Robin, holding up his arms and looking down at himself, "I do think it be somewhat of a gaudy grasshopper dress; but it doth not ill befit my looks. But stay, Little John, here are two bags of gold that I would have thee carry in thy pouch." Then gathering his men together in a close rank, in the midst of which were Allan and Friar Tuck, Robin led them forth.

So they walked on for a long time till they came to a certain little church that belonged to the rich Priory of Emmet. Here it was that fair Ellen was to be married. On the other side of the road from where the church stood, with waving fields of barley around, ran a stone wall covered by a mass of blossoming woodbine. Behind the wall, in the tall soft grass, the yeomen sat them down, and glad they were to rest after their long tramp.

"Now," quoth Robin, "I would have young David of Doncaster watch and tell me when he sees anyone coming to the church. So get thee upon the wall, David, and hide beneath the woodbine."

Accordingly young David did as he was bidden. Then all was quiet save only for the low voices of those that talked together, and for the mellow snoring of Friar Tuck, who enjoyed his sleep with a noise as of one sawing soft wood very slowly, and saving also for Allan's restless footsteps pacing up and down, for his soul was so full of disturbance that he could not stand still. And so a long time passed.

Then up spoke Robin, "Now, David, what dost thou see?"

Then David answered, "I see three black crows flying over the wold; but naught else do I see, good master."

So another time passed till Robin, growing impatient, spoke again. "Now tell me, David, what dost thou see by this?"

And David answered, "I see the windmills swinging and three tall poplar trees swaying against the sky; but naught else do I see."

So another time passed, till Robin asked young David once more what he saw; and David said, "I see how the wind makes waves in the barley field; and now over the hill to the church cometh an old friar, and he carries a great bunch of keys."

Then Robin shook Friar Tuck awake. "Come, rouse thee, holy man!" cried he. "For yonder is one of thy cloth. Go, get thee into the church, that thou may'st be there when thou art wanted."

So with much grunting the stout Friar Tuck clambered over the wall and came to the church where the old friar was laboring with the key, the lock being rusty and he somewhat feeble.

"Halloa, brother," quoth Tuck, "let me aid thee." So saying, he took the key from the other's hand and quickly opened the door.

"Who art thou, brother?" asked the old friar, in a high, wheezing voice. And he blinked at Tuck like an owl at the sun.

"My name is Tuck," said the other, "and I come from Fountain Dale. But, if I understand aught, there is to be a wedding here today and I would fain see this fine sight."

"Truly, thou art welcome, brother," said the old man, leading the way within. Meantime, Robin Hood, in his guise of harper, with Little John and Will Stutely, had come to the church. Robin sat him down on a bench beside the door, but Little John, carrying the bags of gold, went within, as did Will Stutely.

So Robin looked up and down the road till he saw six horsemen come riding sedately. The first was the Bishop of Hereford, and a fine figure he cut. His vestments were of the richest silk, and around his neck was a chain of gold, and around his black velvet cap were rows of jewels that flashed in the sunlight. His hose were of flame-colored silk, and his shoes of black velvet, and on either instep was embroidered a cross in gold thread. Beside the Bishop rode the Prior of Emmet upon a mincing palfrey. Rich were his clothes also, but not so gay as the Bishop's. Behind these were two of the higher brethren of Emmet, and behind these again two retainers belonging to the Bishop; for the Lord Bishop strove to be as like the great barons as was in his power.

When Robin saw this train drawing near, quoth he to himself, Yon Bishop is overgaudy for a holy man. I do wonder whether his patron, Saint Thomas, was given to wearing golden chains, silk clothing and pointed shoes, the money for which, God wot, hath been wrung from the sweat of poor tenants. Bishop, Bishop, thy pride may have a fall ere thou wottest of it.

So the holy men came to the church and dismounted; and the Bishop caught sight of Robin. "Halloa, good fellow," quoth he in a jovial voice, "who art thou that struttest in such gay feathers?"

"A harper am I from the north country," quoth Robin, "and I can touch the strings, I wot, as never another man in all merry England. Many a knight and burgher have danced to my music, and most times greatly against their will; such is the magic of my harping. Now, my Lord Bishop, if I may play at this wedding, I will cause the fair bride to love the man she marries with a love that shall last as long as that twain shall live."

"Ha! Is it so?" cried the Bishop. "Now, if thou wilt cause this maiden (who hath verily bewitched my poor cousin Stephen) thus to love, I will give thee whatsoever thou wilt ask me in due measure. Look, Prior, hither cometh our cousin and his ladylove."

And now, around the bend of the road, came riding Sir Stephen, a tall, thin man, dressed in black silk, with a black velvet cap upon his head. Beside him rode a stout Saxon franklin, Ellen's father, Edward of Deirwold; behind those two came a litter borne by

45

two horses, and therein was a maiden. Behind this litter rode six men-at-arms, the sunlight flashing on their steel caps. So these also came to the church, and there Sir Stephen leaped from his horse and handed Ellen out from the litter. She was the fairest maiden that ever Robin had beheld. But she was pale and drooping, like a lily snapped at the stem; and so, with bent head and sorrowful look, she went within the church, Sir Stephen leading her by the hand.

"Why dost thou not play, fellow?" quoth the Bishop, looking sternly at Robin.

"Marry," said Robin calmly, "I will play in greater wise than your lordship thinks; but not till the right time hath come."

And now fair Ellen and Sir Stephen stood before the altar, and the Bishop came in his robes and opened his book, whereat Ellen looked up and about her in bitter despair. Then, in all his fluttering tags and ribbons of red and yellow, Robin Hood strode forward and stood between the bride and bridegroom.

"Let me look upon this lass," he said in a loud voice. "Why, what have we here? Here be lilies in the cheeks, and not roses such as befit a bonny bride. This is no fit wedding. Thou, Sir Knight, so old, and she so young. I tell thee it may not be, for thou art not her own true love."

At this everyone looked at Robin as though changed to stone. Then he clapped his horn to his lips and blew three blasts that echoed from floor to rafter, as though sounded by the trump of doom. Then straightway Little John and Will Stutely came leaping and stood on either side of Robin Hood, and quickly drew their broadswords, the while a mighty voice rolled over the heads of all: "Here be I, good master, when thou wantest me"; for it was Friar Tuck that so called from the organ loft.

Stout Edward strode forward raging, and would have dragged his daughter away, but Little John stepped between them. "Stand back, old man," said he, "thou art a hobbled horse this day."

"Down with the villains!" cried Sir Stephen, and felt for his sword, but it hung not beside him on his wedding day.

Then the men-at-arms drew their swords, and it seemed like that blood would wet the stones; but suddenly came a bustle at the door and loud voices, steel flashed in the light, and up the aisle came leaping eighteen stout yeomen clad in Lincoln green, with Allan a Dale at their head. In his hand he bore Robin's yew bow, and this he gave to him, kneeling the while upon one knee.

Then up spoke Edward of Deirwold in a deep voice of anger, "Is it thou, Allan a Dale, that hath bred this coil in a church?"

"Nay," quoth merry Robin, "that have I done, and I care not who knoweth it, for my name is Robin Hood."

At this a sudden silence fell. Those of Emmet gathered together like a flock of frightened sheep when the scent of the wolf is nigh, while the Bishop crossed himself devoutly. "Now heaven keep us this day," said he, "from that evil man!"

"Nay," quoth Robin, "I mean you no harm; but here is fair Ellen's betrothed husband, and she shall marry him."

Then up spoke stout Edward in a loud and angry voice, "Now I say nay! I am her father, and she shall marry Sir Stephen."

"Nay, fellow," said Sir Stephen, "I would not marry thy daughter after this day's doings could I gain all England thereby. I loved her, old as I am, and would have taken her up like a jewel from the sty, yet, truly, I knew not that she did love this fellow, and was beloved by him. Maiden, if thou dost rather choose a beggarly minstrel than a highborn knight, take thy choice." Thus saying, he gathered his men about him and walked proudly down the aisle.

Then the Bishop spoke hastily, "I, too, have no business here, and so will depart." But Robin laid hold of his clothes and held him. "Stay, my Lord Bishop," said he, "I have yet somewhat to say to thee." The Bishop's face fell, but he stayed.

Then Robin Hood turned to stout Edward of Deirwold, and said he, "Give thy blessing on thy daughter's marriage to this yeoman and all will be well. Little John, give me the bags of gold. Look, farmer. Here are two hundred bright golden angels; give thy blessing, as I say, and I will count them out to thee. Give not thy blessing, and she shall be married all the same, but not so much as a cracked farthing shall cross thy palm."

Then Edward looked upon the ground with bent brows; but he was a shrewd man and one, withal, that made the best use of a cracked pipkin; so at last he looked up and said, but in no joyous tone, "If the wench will go her own gait, let her go. I had thought to make a lady of her. Ne'ertheless, I will give her my blessing."

"But the wedding may not be," spoke up one of those of Emmet. "The banns have not been duly published, neither is there any priest here willing to marry them."

"How say'st thou?" roared Tuck from the organ loft. "No priest? Marry, here stands as holy a man as thou art. As for the question of banns, stumble not over that straw, brother, for I will publish them." So saying, he called the banns; and, lest three times should not be enough, he published them nine times o'er. Then he came down from the loft and forthwith performed the marriage service; and so Allan and Ellen were duly wedded.

And now Robin counted out two hundred golden angels to Edward of Deirwold, and he gave his blessing, yet not, I wot, with overmuch goodwill. Then the stout yeomen crowded around and grasped Allan's palm, and he, holding Ellen's hand within his own, looked about him all dizzy with happiness.

Then at last Robin turned to the Bishop. "My Lord Bishop," quoth he, "thou didst promise me that did I play in such wise as to cause this fair lass to love her husband, thou wouldst give me whatsoever I asked in reason. I have played my play, and she loveth her husband, which she would not have done but for me; so now give me, I prithee, thy golden chain as a wedding present for this fair bride."

Then the Bishop's cheeks grew red with rage, but he saw in Robin's face that which bade him pause. Slowly he took the chain from about his neck and handed it to Robin, who flung it over Ellen's head so that it hung glittering about her shoulders.

Now Robin Hood gathered his men together, and, with Allan and his bride, they turned their steps toward the woodlands. On the way Friar Tuck came close to Robin and plucked him by the sleeve. "Thou dost lead a merry life," quoth he, "but dost thou not think it would be for the welfare of all your souls to have a good stout chaplain, such as I, to oversee holy matters?" At this Robin laughed amain, and bade him become one of the band.

That night there was such a feast in the greenwood as Nottinghamshire never saw before. To that feast you and I were not bidden; so, lest we should both feel the matter more keenly, I will say no more about it.

Robin Hood Aids a Sorrowful Knight

SO PASSED THE SUMMER with its quivering heat, its long twilights and its mellow nights, through which the frogs croaked and fairy folk were said to be out on the hillsides. The time of fall had come; now, when the harvest was gathered home, bands of gleaners roamed the country, singing along the roads in the daytime and sleeping beneath hedgerows and hayricks at night. Now the hips burned red in the thickets and the haws waxed black in the hedgerows, the stubble lay all crisp and naked to the sky, and the leaves were fast turning russet and brown.

Quoth Robin, snuffing the air, "Here is a fair day, Little John, and one that we can ill waste in idleness. Choose such men as thou dost need, and go thou east while I will wend to the west, and see that each of us bringeth back some goodly guest to dine beneath the greenwood tree."

"Marry," cried Little John, clapping his palms together for joy, "I'll bring thee a guest, or come not back mine own self."

Now, you and I cannot go two ways at the same time, so we will e'en let Little John and his men follow their own path while we trudge after Robin. And here is good company: Robin Hood, Will Scarlet, Allan a Dale, Midge, the Miller's son, and others.

Robin followed his fancy and the others followed Robin. Passing by fair Mansfield Town, with its towers and battlements and spires all smiling in the sun, they came at last out of the forest lands. Onward they journeyed, until they came over beyond Alverton in Derbyshire. By this time high noontide had come; so, coming to a shrine at the crossing of two roads, Robin called upon them to stop, for on either side was shelter of high hedgerows, behind which they could watch the roads. Here, where the grass was soft, they sat them down. Then each drew from his pouch that which he had brought to eat. In front of them, one of the roads crawled up the steep hill and then dipped suddenly over its crest. Over the top of the hill showed a windmill, the sails slowly rising and dipping against the clear blue sky as the light wind moved them with creaking and labored swing.

After a time, a man came riding over the hill and down the road toward where Robin and his band lay hidden. No chain of gold hung around his neck, and no jewel was about him; yet no one could mistake him for aught but one of proud and noble blood. But his head was bowed and his hands drooped limp on either side; and even his horse, the reins loose upon his neck, walked with hanging head, as though he shared his master's grief.

Quoth Robin, "Yon is verily a sorry-looking gallant; nevertheless, there may be some pickings. Bide ye here till I look into this matter." So, when the knight came riding slowly along, Robin stepped forward and laid his hand upon the bridle rein.

"What art thou, friend, who dost stop a traveler in this manner upon his most gracious Majesty's highway?" said the knight.

"Marry," quoth Robin, "that is hard to answer. One man calleth me kind, another cruel; this one calleth me honest fellow, and that one, vile thief. Truly, the world hath as many eyes to look upon a man as there are spots on a toad; with what eyes thou regardest me lieth with thine own self. My name is Robin Hood."

"Truly," said the knight, a smile twitching at the corners of his mouth, "thou hast a quaint conceit. As for the eyes with which I regard thee, they are as favorable as may be, for I hear much good of thee and little ill. What is thy will of me?"

"Now, I make my vow, Sir Knight," quoth Robin, "thou hast spoken fair words. If thou wilt go with me this day to Sherwood Forest, I will give thee a merry feast. We keep an inn, as it were, but so far from highroads that guests do not often come nigh us; so I and my friends set off merrily and seek them when we grow dull of ourselves. Yet I will furthermore tell thee, Sir Knight, that we count upon our guests paying a reckoning." Then, still holding the horse by the bridle rein, he put his fingers to his lips and blew a shrill whistle, whereupon fourscore yeomen came running to where he stood. "These," said Robin, "are some of my merry men. They share and share alike with me all joys and troubles, gains and losses. Now, Sir Knight, I prithee tell me what money thou hast about thee."

A slow red arose into the knight's cheeks, and he said, "I know not why I should be ashamed; but, friend, I pledge my knightly word that in my purse are ten shillings, and that that is every groat that Sir Richard of the Lea hath in all the world." And he held his purse out to Robin.

"Put up thy purse, Sir Richard," quoth Robin. "Far be it from me to doubt the word of so gentle a knight. The proud I strive to bring low, but those that walk in sorrow I would aid if I could. Come, Sir Richard, go with us to the greenwood. I may perchance aid thee, if thou dost find it in thy heart to tell me of thy sorrows."

"Truly, friend," said Sir Richard, "methinks thou meanest kindness; nevertheless my troubles are such that it is not likely thou canst cure them. But I will go with thee."

As they traveled, the knight spoke of his sorrows thus: "My castle and my lands are in pawn for a debt. Three days hence the money must be paid or else all mine estate falls into the hands of the Priory of Emmet."

Quoth Robin, "I understand not why those of thy kind live in such a manner that all their wealth passeth from them like snow beneath the springtide sun."

"Thou wrongest me, Robin," said the knight, "for listen: I have a son but twenty winters old. Last year the jousts were held at Chester, and thither my son went, as did I and my lady wife. I wot it was a proud time for us, for he unhorsed each knight that he tilted against. At last he ran a course with a great knight, Sir Walter of Lancaster. My son kept his seat, albeit both spears were shivered to the haft; but a splinter of my boy's lance ran through the visor of Sir Walter's helmet, so that he died. Sir Walter had great friends at court, so, to save my son from prison, I had to pay a ransom of six hundred pounds. All might have gone well even yet, only that, by ins and outs and crookedness of laws, I was shorn like a sheep. I had to pawn my lands to the Priory of Emmet, and a hard bargain they drove."

"But where is thy son now?" asked Robin.

"In Palestine," said Sir Richard, "battling like a brave Christian soldier for the Cross and the Holy Sepulcher. England was an ill place for him because of the hate of Sir Walter's kinsmen."

"Truly," said Robin, much moved, "thine is a hard lot. But tell me, what is owing to Emmet for thine estates?"

"Only four hundred pounds," said Sir Richard.

At this, Robin smote his thigh in anger. "Oh the bloodsuckers!" cried he. "A noble estate to be forfeit for four hundred pounds!"

"Yet it is not mine own lot that doth trouble me," said the knight, "but my dear lady's; for should I lose my land she will have to betake herself to some kinsman and there abide in charity. As for me, I will go to Palestine to join my son."

Then up spoke Will Scarlet, "But hast thou no friend that will help thee in thy dire need?"

"Never a man," said Sir Richard. "While I was rich enow, I had friends. But when the oak falls in the forest the swine run from beneath it lest they should be smitten down also."

Then Robin said, "Thou say'st thou hast no friends. I make no boast, but many have found Robin Hood a friend in their troubles. Cheer up, Sir Richard, I may help thee yet."

The day was well-nigh gone when they came to the greenwood tree, and whom should they find that Little John had brought but the Lord Bishop of Hereford! Up and down the Bishop walked like a fox caught in a hen coop. Behind him were three Black Friars standing close together, like three black sheep in a tempest. Hitched to the trees close at hand were six horses, one of them a barb with gay trappings upon which the Bishop was wont to ride, and the others laden with divers packs.

When the Bishop saw Robin he made as though he would have run toward the yeoman, but the fellow that guarded him thrust his quarterstaff in front, so that his lordship was fain to stand back.

"Stay, my Lord Bishop," cried Robin. "I will come to thee with all speed, for I would rather see thee than any man in England."

"How now," quoth the Bishop in an angry voice, "is this the way thy band treats the Church? I and these brethren were passing peacefully along the highroad with a halfscore of guards, when up comes a fellow full seven feet high, with fourscore or more men back of him, and calls upon me to stop—me, the Lord Bishop of Hereford! Whereupon my guards—beshrew them for cowards!—straight ran away. But look ye; not only did this fellow stop me, but he called me such vile names as fat priest, man-eating bishop and money-gorging usurer."

"Alas! my lord," said Robin, "that thou hast been so ill-treated! Little John, didst thou call his lordship a fat priest?"

"Aye," said Little John sorrowfully.

"And a man-eating bishop, and a money-gorging usurer?"

"Aye," said Little John, more sorrowfully than before.

"Alas, that these things should be!" said Robin, turning to the Bishop. "For I have ever found Little John a truthful man."

At this, a roar of laughter went up, whereat the blood rushed into the Bishop's face till it was cherry-red; but he swallowed his words, though they well-nigh choked him.

"Nay, my Lord Bishop," said Robin, "we are rough fellows, but there is not a man here that would harm a hair of thy reverence's head. Come, my merry men, get the feast ready."

Then, when the feast was spread, Robin brought forward Sir Richard of the Lea. "My Lord Bishop," said he, "here is another guest that we have with us this day. I wish that thou mightest know him better." Then Robin bade his guests be seated. "I have a story to tell you all, so listen to what I have to say," quoth he. Then the Bishop's heart sank within him with grim forebodings, as he told them all about Sir Richard, and how his lands were in pawn. "Now, my Lord Bishop," said Robin, "dost thou not think this is ill done of anyone, much more of a churchman, who should live in charity? And, as thou art the richest bishop in all England, canst thou not help this needy brother?"

To this the Bishop answered not a word but looked upon the ground with moody eyes.

Then Robin said to Little John, "Go thou and Will Stutely and bring forth those packhorses yonder." Then asked he of the friars, "Who hath the score of the goods?"

Then up spoke the smallest of the Black Friars in a trembling voice—an old man he was, with a gentle, wrinkled face. "That have I; but, I pray thee, harm me not."

"Nay," quoth Robin, "I have never harmed harmless man yet; but give it to me, good father." So the old man handed Robin the tablet on which was marked down the account of the various packs. This Robin handed to Will Scarlet, bidding him to read the same. So Will began:

"*Three bales of silk to Quentin, the mercer at Ancaster.*"

"That we touch not," quoth Robin, "for this Quentin is an honest fellow, who hath risen by his own thrift."

"*One bale of silk velvet for the Abbey of Beaumont.*"

"What do priests want of silk velvet?" quoth Robin. "Nevertheless, I will not take all. Measure it off into three lots, one to be sold for charity, one for us, and one for the abbey."

"*Twoscore of wax candles for the Chapel of Saint Thomas.*"

"They belong fairly to Saint Thomas," said Robin. So the list was gone through, and the goods adjudged according to what Robin thought fit; and so they came to the last line upon the tablet—"*A box belonging to the Lord Bishop of Hereford.*"

At these words the Bishop shook as with a chill, and a box heavily bound with bands of iron was set upon the ground.

"My Lord Bishop, hast thou the key of this box?" asked Robin. The Bishop shook his head.

"Will Scarlet," said Robin, "cut this box open." Then up rose Will Scarlet and he smote that ironbound box with a great two-handed sword. At the third blow it burst open and a heap of gold came rolling forth, gleaming red in the torchlight. At this sight a murmur went all around among the band.

Quoth Robin, "Thou, Will Scarlet, thou, Allan a Dale, and thou, Little John, count it over."

When all the money had been scored up, Will Scarlet called out that there were fifteen hundred golden pounds. But among the gold they found a paper, and this he read in a loud voice, that this money was the rental and forfeits from estates belonging to the Bishopric of Hereford.

"My Lord Bishop," said Robin Hood, "thou shalt take back one third of thy money. One third of it thou canst well spare to us for thy entertainment; and one third of it for Sir Richard of the Lea. The Church seemed like to despoil Sir Richard, therefore some of the overplus of Church gains may well be used in aiding him."

Sir Richard looked at Robin until something arose in his eyes that made all the lights and the faces blur together. At last he said, "I thank thee, friend, from my heart; yet, think not ill if I cannot take thy gift freely. But I will take the money and pay my debts, and in a year and a day hence will return it safe either to thee or to the Lord Bishop of Hereford. For this I pledge my most solemn knightly word. I feel free to borrow, for I know no man that should be more bound to aid me than one so high in that church that hath driven such a hard bargain."

"Sir Knight," quoth Robin, "it shall be as thou dost wish. But thou hadst best bring the money to me at the end of the year, for mayhap I may make better use of it than the Bishop." Thereupon he ordered that five hundred pounds be tied up in a leathern bag for Sir Richard.

Then Sir Richard arose. "I cannot stay later, good friends," said he, "for my lady will wax anxious if I come not home."

Then up spoke Will Stutely, "Let us give Sir Richard yon bale of rich velvet to take to his noble lady."

At this all clapped their hands for joy, and Robin said, "Thou hast well spoken, and it shall be done."

Then Sir Richard of the Lea said in a husky, trembling voice, "Ye shall all see, good friends, that Sir Richard o' the Lea will ever remember your kindness this day. And if ye be at any time in dire trouble, come to me and my lady, and the walls of Castle Lea shall be battered down ere harm shall befall you."

But now Little John led forward Sir Richard's horse, and the knight mounted. He looked down at Robin for a little time, then stooped and kissed his cheek; and all the forest glades rang with the shout that went up as the knight rode off.

Then up spoke the Bishop of Hereford in a mournful voice, "I, too, must be jogging, good fellow, for the night waxes late."

"Be not so hasty, Lord Bishop," said Robin. "Three days hence Sir Richard must pay his debts to Emmet; until that time thou must abide with me. I promise thee that thou shalt have great sport, for I know thou art fond of hunting the dun deer."

So the Bishop and his train abided with Robin for three days, and much sport his lordship had in that time, so he was sorry when the time came to go. And Robin sent him forth, with a guard to keep freebooters from taking what was left of the packs. But, as the Bishop rode away, he vowed within himself that he would make Robin rue the day that he stopped him in Sherwood.

THE AFTERNOON SUN was streaming in through the arched windows of the refectory at Emmet Priory; it lay in broad squares of light upon the stone floor and across the board covered with a snowy linen cloth. At the head of the table sat Prior Vincent of Emmet all clad in soft robes of fine cloth; on his head was a black velvet cap picked out with gold, and around his neck hung a heavy chain of gold, with a great locket pendant therefrom. On the arm of his chair roosted his favorite falcon. On his right hand sat the Sheriff of Nottingham in robes of purple trimmed with fur, and on his left a famous doctor of law in dark and sober garb.

The wizened face of the man of law was twisted into a wrinkled smile, for in his pouch were fourscore golden angels that the Prior had paid him in fee for the case betwixt him and Sir Richard of the Lea. The learned doctor had been paid beforehand, for he had not overmuch trust in the holy Vincent of Emmet.

Quoth the Sheriff of Nottingham, "But art thou sure, Sir Prior, that thou hast the lands so safe?"

"Aye, marry," said Prior Vincent, smacking his lips after a deep draught of wine, "I have kept a close watch upon Sir Richard and I know right well that he hath no money to pay me withal."

"Aye, true," said the man of law in a dry, husky voice, "and his land is surely forfeit if he cometh not to pay this day."

But even as the doctor spoke, there came a sudden clatter of horses' hoofs and a jingle of iron mail in the courtyard below.

Then a door at the lower end of the refectory swung open, and in came Sir Richard, with folded hands, and head bowed upon his breast. Thus humbly he walked up the hall, while his men-at-arms stood about the door. When he had come to where the Prior sat, he knelt upon one knee. "Save and keep thee, Sir Prior," said he, "I am come to keep my day."

"Hast thou brought my money?" the Prior said.

"Alas! I have not so much as a penny upon me," said the knight. "As thou hopest for heaven's mercy, show mercy to me. Strip me not of my lands and so reduce a true knight to poverty."

"Thy day is broken and thy lands forfeit," said the man of law, while the Prior's eyes sparkled.

Still the knight knelt upon the hard stone. "Wilt thou not be my friend, Sir Sheriff?" said he.

"Nay," quoth the Sheriff, "this is no business of mine; yet . . . wilt thou not ease him of some of his debts, Sir Prior?"

At this the Prior smiled grimly. "Pay me three hundred pounds, Sir Richard," said he, "and I will give thee quittance of thy debt."

"Thou knowest, Sir Prior, that it is as easy for me to pay four hundred pounds as three hundred," said Sir Richard. "But wilt thou not give me another twelvemonth to pay my debt?"

"Not another day," cried the Prior. "Either pay thy debt as I have said, or release thy land and get thee gone."

Then Sir Richard arose to his feet. "Thou false priest! Hast thou so little courtesy that thou wouldst see a true knight kneel for all this time, and never offer him meat or drink?"

Then turning to his men-at-arms, he called, "Come hither"; whereupon the tallest came forward and handed him a leathern bag. Sir Richard took the bag and shot from it upon the table a glittering stream of golden money. "Bear in mind, Sir Prior," said he, "that thou hast promised me quittance for three hundred pounds. Not one farthing above that shalt thou get." So saying, he counted out three hundred pounds and pushed it toward the Prior.

But now the Prior's hands dropped at his sides and his head hung upon his shoulder, for not only had he lost all hopes of the land, but he had forgiven the knight one hundred pounds of his debt and had paid the man of law fourscore angels. To him he turned, and quoth he, "Give me back my money that thou hast."

"Nay," cried the other shrilly, "it is but my fee that thou didst pay me." And he hugged his gown about him.

"Sir Prior," quoth Sir Richard, "I have paid my dues; there is no more betwixt us." So saying, he turned and strode away.

Now a twelvemonth and a day passed since Prior Vincent sat at feast, and once more the mellow fall had come. But the year had brought great change to the lands of Sir Richard of the Lea; for, where before shaggy wild grasses grew, now all stretched away in golden stubble. In the castle, also, where were empty moats and the crumbling of neglect, all was now orderly and well kept.

Bright shone the sun on battlement and tower, and in the blue air overhead a flock of clattering jackdaws flew around the gilded weather vane and spire. Then the drawbridge fell across the moat with a rattle and clank of chains, the gate of the castle swung open, and a goodly array of steel-clad men-at-arms, with a knight all clothed in chain mail, as white as frost on brier of a winter morning, came flashing out from the castle courtyard. In his hand the knight held a great spear, from the point of which fluttered a blood-red pennant. And in the midst of the troop walked three packhorses laden with parcels of divers shapes. Thus rode forth good Sir Richard of the Lea to pay his debt to Robin Hood.

As they marched onward, Robin stood in the greenwood with his stout yeomen around him, awaiting Sir Richard's coming. At last a glint of steel was seen through the brown forest leaves, and into the open rode Sir Richard at the head of his men.

"Why, how now," said Robin, "methinks thou art a gayer bird than when I saw thee last."

"Yes, thanks to thee, Robin," said the knight, leaping from his horse and laying his hand upon the yeoman's shoulder. "But for thee I would now have been wandering in misery in a far country. But I have brought back the money that thou didst lend me, and which I have doubled four times over again, and so become rich

once more. Along with this money I have brought a gift to thee
and thy brave men from my dear lady and myself." Then one of
the men brought the knight a strongbox from which he took a
bag and counted out five hundred pounds.

Then Sir Richard had the packs opened and lo, there were tenscore bows of finest Spanish yew, all inlaid with fanciful figures in
silver. Beside these were tenscore quivers of leather embroidered
with golden thread, and in each quiver were a score of shafts with
burnished heads; each shaft was feathered with peacock's plumes,
nocked with silver. Sir Richard gave to each yeoman a bow and a
quiver of arrows, but to Robin he gave a stout bow inlaid with the
cunningest workmanship in gold, while each arrow in his quiver
was nocked with gold. Then all swore that they would die if need
be for Sir Richard and his lady.

At last, after a merry feast, the time came for Sir Richard to go,
whereupon each of the yeomen took a torch to light the way
through the forest. So they came to the edge of Sherwood, and
there the knight kissed Robin upon his cheek and left him.

Little John Turns Barefoot Friar

COLD WINTER HAD PASSED and spring had come again. The budding leaves hung like a tender mist about the trees, and in the open
country the cornfields were thick and soft with growing blades.
The plowboy shouted in the sun, and in the new-turned furrows
flocks of birds hunted for fat worms.

On a deer's hide, stretched out in front of the greenwood tree,
sat Robin Hood basking in the sun. Leaning back with his hands
clasped about his knees, he lazily watched Little John rolling a
stout bowstring from long strands of hempen thread, wetting the
palms of his hands ever and anon, and rolling the cord upon his
thigh. Nearby sat Allan a Dale fitting a new string to his harp.

Quoth Robin, "Methinks I would rather roam this forest than
be king of all merry England."

"Yea," quoth Little John, as he rubbed his new-made bowstring with yellow beeswax, "the life we lead is the life for me. Even the winter hath its joys. Dost thou remember that night thou and Friar Tuck and I passed at the Blue Boar with the two beggars and the strolling friar?"

"Yea," quoth Robin, "that was a goodly song that the strolling friar sang. Friar Tuck, thou hast a quick ear for a tune. Dost thou remember it?"

"Let me see," said Tuck, and he touched his forefinger to his forehead in thought, humming to himself, and stopping ever and anon to fit what he had got to what he searched for in his mind. At last he cleared his throat and sang in a mellow voice:

> *"Good is the life of the strolling friar,*
> *With aplenty to eat and to drink;*
> *For the goodwife will keep him a seat by the fire,*
> *And the pretty girls smile at his wink.*
> *Then he lustily trolls,*
> *As he onward strolls,*
> *A rollicking song for the saving of souls.*
> *When the wind doth blow,*
> *With the coming of snow,*
> *There's a place by the fire*
> *For the fatherly friar,*
> *And a crab in the bowl for his heart's desire."*

"It is a goodly song," quoth Little John, "and, were I not a yeoman of Sherwood Forest, fain would I be a strolling friar."

"Yea," said Robin, "but methought those two burly beggars led a merrier life. What say'st thou, Little John, to an adventure? Don thou a friar's gown from our chest of strange garments, and I will stop the first beggar I meet and change clothes with him. Then let us wander the country about, and see what befalls us."

"That fitteth my mind well," quoth Little John.

Thereupon Little John went to the storehouse of the band, and chose the robe of a Gray Friar. When he came forth again, a mighty roar of laughter went up, for the robe was too short for him by a good palm's breadth. But Little John's hands were folded

But the stranger turned the blow right deftly and in return gave one as stout, which Robin turned also.

"Now stand thou back thine own self," quoth Little John, and smote the man a buffet beside his head that felled him as a butcher fells an ox, and then he leaped to the cart.

So Robin took his sword again and buckled it at his side; then he bent his stout back and took the friar on it.

"Will Scarlet," said Robin, "cut this box open."

"Thine eggs are cracked, Gilbert," quoth Robin, laughing; and once more he smote the white circle of the center.

Little John twanged his bowstring with a shout, and when the sheriff dashed in through the gates of Nottingham Town it was with a gray goose shaft sticking out behind him, like a molting sparrow with one feather in its tail.

HOWARD PYLE

in his sleeves, and Little John's eyes were cast upon the ground, and at his girdle hung a long string of beads.

And now Little John took up his stout staff, at the end of which hung a little leathern bottle, such as palmers carry; but in it was something, I wot, more like good malmsey than cold spring water, such as godly pilgrims carry. Then up rose Robin and took his stout staff in his hand, likewise, and slipped ten golden angels into his pouch, and the two yeomen set forth. They walked down the forest path and then along the highway till it split in twain.

Quoth Robin, "Take thou this road, and I will take that. So, fare thee well, holy father, and may'st thou not ha' cause to count thy beads in earnest ere we meet again."

"Good den, good beggar that is to be," quoth Little John. "May'st thou have no cause to beg for mercy ere I see thee next."

Up hill and down dale walked Little John, the fresh wind blowing in his face and his robes fluttering behind, and at last he came to a crossroad. Here he met three pretty lasses, each bearing a basket of eggs. Quoth he, "Whither away, fair maids?"

Then they huddled together and nudged one another, and one said, "We are going to the Tuxford market, holy friar."

"Now out upon it!" quoth Little John. "Surely, it is a pity that such fair lasses should be forced to carry eggs to market. An I had the shaping of things in this world, ye should all have been clothed in silk, and ride upon milk-white horses, and feed upon nothing but whipped cream and strawberries."

At this speech the pretty maids blushed and simpered. One said, "La!" another, "Marry, a' maketh sport of us!" and the third, "Listen, now, to the holy man!"

"Now, look you," said Little John, "I cannot see such dainty damsels carrying baskets along a highroad. Let me take them, and one of you may carry my staff for me."

"Nay," said one of the lasses, "but thou canst not carry three baskets all at one time."

"Yea, but I can," said Little John. "Look ye, now. Here I take this great basket, so; here I tie my rosary around the handle, thus; and here I slip the rosary over my head and sling the basket upon my back, in this wise." And the basket hung down behind him like a peddler's pack; then, giving his staff to one of the maids, and taking a basket upon either arm, he stepped forth merrily toward Tuxford Town, a pretty maid on either side, and one walking ahead, carrying the staff. In this wise they journeyed along, and everyone they met stopped and looked after them, laughing.

When they came nigh to Tuxford, Little John set down the baskets, for he did not care to meet some of the Sheriff's men. "Alas! sweet chucks," quoth he, "here I must leave you. Now, ere we part, we must drink sweet friendship." So saying, he unslung the leathern bottle from the end of his staff, and, drawing the stopper therefrom, he handed it to the lass who had carried his staff. Then each lass took a fair drink of what was within, and Little John finished what was left. Then, kissing each lass sweetly, he wished them all good den, and left them. But the maids stood looking after him as he walked away whistling. "What a pity," quoth one, "that such a lusty lad should be in holy orders."

"Marry," quoth Little John, as he strode along, "yon was no such ill happening; Saint Dunstan send me more of the like."

After a time he began to wax thirsty again in the warmth of the day. He shook his leathern bottle beside his ear, but not a sound came therefrom! Then he placed it to his lips and tilted it aloft, but not a drop was there. Little John, Little John, said he sadly to himself, woman will be thy ruin yet!

At last he came to a little inn. Beside the door stood two stout cobs with broad soft-padded saddles, speaking of rich guests. In front of the door three merry fellows, a tinker, a peddler and a beggar, were seated on a bench in the sun quaffing ale.

"I give you good den, sweet friends," quoth Little John.

"Give thee good den, holy father," quoth the beggar. "But look thee, thy gown is too short. Thou hadst best cut a piece off the top and tack it to the bottom. But come, sit beside us and take a taste of ale, if thy vows forbid thee not."

"Nay," quoth Little John, "the blessed Saint Dunstan hath given me a dispensation for all indulgence in that line."

"Truly," quoth the tinker, "without thy looks belie thee, holy friar, the good Saint Dunstan was wise, for without such dispensation his votary is like to ha' many a penance to make. Ho, landlord, a pot of ale!"

So the ale was brought and given to Little John. Then, blowing the froth a little way to make room for his lips, he tilted the bottom of the pot higher and higher till it pointed to the sky, and he had to shut his eyes to keep the dazzle of the sunshine out of them. Then he heaved a full deep sigh.

"Ho, landlord!" cried the peddler. "Bring this good fellow another pot of ale, for truly it is a credit to us all to have one among us who can empty a cannikin so lustily."

So they talked among themselves merrily, until after a while quoth Little John, "Who rideth those two nags yonder?"

"Two holy men like thee, brother, from Fountain Abbey, in Yorkshire," quoth the beggar. "They are now having a goodly feast within. But come, good friar, has not thy holy Saint Dunstan taught thee a song or two?"

"Why," quoth Little John, grinning, "mayhap he lent me aid to learn a ditty or so." And, after a word or two about a certain hoarseness that troubled him, he sang thus:

> "*Ah, pretty, pretty maid, whither dost thou go?*
> *I prithee, prithee, wait for thy lover also,*
> > *And we'll gather the rose*
> > *As it sweetly blows,*
> *For the merry, merry winds are blo-o-o-wing.*"

Now he had got no farther than this when out of the inn came the two brothers of Fountain Abbey. The one was as fat as a suet pudding, the other lean as an old wife's spindle. When they saw who it was that sang, the fat little brother drew his heavy eyebrows together. "How, now," he roared, his voice coming from him like loud thunder from a little cloud, "is this a fit place for one in thy garb to tipple and sing profane songs?"

"Nay," quoth Little John, "sin' I cannot tipple and sing, like your worship's reverence, in such a goodly place as Fountain Abbey, I must e'en tipple and sing where I can."

"Now, out upon thee," cried the thin brother, "that thou shouldst so disgrace thy cloth by this talk and bearing."

"Marry," quoth Little John, "methinks it is more disgrace to wring hard-earned farthings out of poor lean peasants."

The tinker and the peddler and the beggar nudged one another, and the friars scowled blackly; but they could think of nothing further to say, so they turned to their horses. Then Little John arose. "Truly, your words have smitten my sinful heart," quoth he. "I will abide no longer in this den of evil, but will go with you. No vile temptation will fall upon me in such holy company."

Now, at this all the good fellows on the bench grinned till their teeth glistened. As for the friars, they knew not what to do. It made them feel sick with shame to think of riding along the high-road with a strolling friar, in robes all too short for him. Then up spoke the fat brother, but more mildly than before. "Nay, good brother," said he, "we will ride fast, and thou wilt tire to death at the pace."

"Truly, I am grateful to thee for the thought," quoth Little John, "but have no fear, brother; my limbs are stout."

So the two brethren, as they could do naught else, mounted their nags, turned their noses toward Lincoln and rode away.

"Off we go, we three," quoth Little John, as he pushed in betwixt the two cobs. And swinging his stout staff over his shoulder, he trudged off, measuring his pace with that of the two nags.

The two brothers drew as far away from Little John as they could, so that he walked in the middle of the road while they rode on the footpath on either side. As they so went away, the tinker, the peddler and the beggar ran skipping out into the highway, each with a pot in his hand, and looked after them laughing.

While they were in sight of those at the inn, the brothers walked their horses soberly, not caring to make ill matters worse by seeming to run away from Little John; but when they had crossed the crest of the hill, quoth the fat brother to the thin brother, "Brother Ambrose, had we not better mend our pace?"

"Why truly," spoke up Little John, "methinks it would be well to boil our pot a little faster, for the day is passing on."

At this the two friars glared on Little John with baleful looks, and clucked to their horses. Both broke into a canter, and for a mile and more Little John ran betwixt them as lightly as a stag. At last the fat brother drew his horse's rein with a groan, for he could stand the shaking no longer. "Alas," said Little John, with not so much as a catch in his breath, "I did sadly fear that the pace would shake thy poor old fat paunch."

At this the fat friar stared straight before him and gnawed his nether lip. And now they traveled forward more quietly. Presently they met three minstrels, who stared amain at so strange a sight.

"Make way!" Little John cried, waving his staff. "For here we go, we three!" Then how the minstrels laughed! But the fat friar shook as with an ague, and the lean friar bowed his head over his horse's neck.

Next they met two knights in rich array, with hawk on wrist, and two fair ladies in silks and velvets, all a-riding on noble steeds. These all made room, staring, and Little John bowed humbly. "Give you greetings, lords and ladies," said he. "But here we go, Big Jack, Lean Jack, and Fat Jack-pudding." The ladies laughed, and the fat friar seemed as if he were like to fall from his saddle for shame; the other brother looked grimly before him.

Soon they came to a crossroad. "Look ye, fellow," quoth the lean friar, in a voice quivering with rage, "we care no longer to be made sport of. Go thy way, and let us go ours in peace."

"La there!" quoth Little John. "Methought we were such a merry company, and I can ill spare you, for I am a poor man and ye are rich. I pray you, brothers, give me a penny or two to buy me bread and cheese at the next inn."

"We have no money, fellow," said the lean friar harshly.

"Ha' ye, in holy truth, no money?" Little John asked. "Then get both of you down from off your horses, and we will kneel here in the middle of the crossroads and pray the blessed Saint Dunstan to send us some money to carry us on our journey."

"Thou limb of evil," cried the lean friar, "dost thou bid me, the high cellarer of Fountain Abbey, to kneel in the dirty road to pray to some beggarly Saxon saint?"

"Now," quoth Little John, "I ha' part of a mind to crack thy head for thee for speaking thus of the good Saint Dunstan! But get down straightway; my patience will not last much longer." So saying, he twirled his staff till it whistled.

At this both friars grew as pale as dough, and down they slipped from off their horses.

"Now, brothers, down on your knees and pray," said Little John; thereupon, putting his heavy hands upon the shoulder of each, he forced them to their knees, he kneeling also. Then Little John began to pray, somewhat in this wise: "O gracious Saint Dunstan! Send some money straightway to these poor folk; but send them only ten shillings apiece, lest they grow puffed up with pride. Any more than that that thou sendest, send to me."

"Now," quoth he, rising, "let us see what each man hath." Then he thrust his hand into his own pouch and drew thence four golden angels. "What have ye, brothers?" said he.

Then each friar slowly thrust his hand into his pouch, and brought it out with nothing in it.

"Have ye nothing?" quoth Little John. "Nay, I warrant there is somewhat that hath crept into the seams of your pouches, and so ye ha' missed it. Let me look." So he went first to the lean friar, and, thrusting his hand into the pouch, he drew forth a leathern bag and counted therefrom one hundred and ten pounds of golden money. Then he thrust his hand into the pouch of the fat friar and drew thence a bag like the other and counted out from it threescore and ten pounds. "Look ye now," quoth he, "I knew the good saint had sent some pittance ye had missed."

Then, giving them one pound between them, he slipped the rest into his own pouch, saying, "Ye pledged me your word that ye had no money. Therefore I know the good Saint Dunstan hath sent this. But as I only prayed for ten shillings to be sent to each of you, all over and above belongeth by rights to me. I give you good den, brothers." The friars looked at one another woefully, and sadly they mounted their horses and rode away.

But Little John turned his footsteps back again to Sherwood Forest, and merrily he whistled as he strode along.

AFTER ROBIN HAD LEFT Little John at the forking of the roads, he walked merrily onward for a long distance until he came to where a stout fellow was sitting upon a stile, swinging his legs. All about this lusty rogue dangled pouches and bags of different sizes and kinds, with great, gaping mouths, like a brood of hungry daws. His coat was patched with as many colors as there are stripes upon a maypole, and on his head he wore a tall leathern cap. Across his knees rested a heavy quarterstaff of blackthorn. His eyes twinkled with merriment, and as jolly a beggar was he as ever trod the lanes of Nottinghamshire.

"Halloa, good fellow," quoth Robin, "what art thou doing here this merry day?"

Then the other winked one eye and straightway trolled forth:

> "*I sit upon the stile,*
> *And I sing a little while*
> *As I wait for my own true dear, O,*
> *For the sun is shining bright,*
> *And the leaves are dancing light,*
> *And the little fowl sings she is near, O.*

And so it is with me, bully boy, saving that my doxy cometh not."

"Now that is a right sweet song," quoth Robin, "and, were I in the mind to listen, I could bear well to hear more; but I have two things of seriousness to ask of thee. First, I have come a long way and fain would know where I shall get somewhat to eat and drink."

"Marry," quoth the beggar, "I make no such serious thoughts upon the matter. I eat when I can get it, and munch my crust when I can get no crumb; likewise, when there is no ale to be had I wash the dust from my throat with water."

"Now, in good sooth," quoth Robin, laughing, "hast thou truly naught but a dry crust about thee? Methinks thy bags and pouches are fat and lusty for such thin fare."

"Why, mayhap there is some other cold fare therein," said the beggar slyly.

"And hast thou naught to drink but cold water?" said Robin.

"Never so much as a drop," quoth the beggar. "Over beyond yon clump of trees is a sweet inn, but I go no more thither. Once, when the good Prior of Emmet was dining there, the landlady set a dear little tart upon the windowsill to cool, and I, fearing it might be lost, took it with me till I could find the owner. Since then they have acted very ill toward me; yet truth bids me say that they have the best ale there that ever rolled over my tongue."

"Marry," quoth Robin, "they did ill toward thee for thy kindness. But tell me truly, what hast thou in thy pouches?"

"Why," quoth the beggar, peeping into the mouths of his bags, "I find here a piece of pigeon pie, wrapped in a cabbage leaf to hold the gravy. Here I behold four oaten cakes and a cold knuckle of ham. Insooth, 'tis strange; but I find six eggs that must have come by accident from some poultry yard hereabout. Roasted upon the coals and spread with a piece of butter that I see—"

"Peace, good friend!" cried Robin. "Thou makest my poor stomach quake with joy. If thou wilt give me to eat, I will straightway hie me to that inn and bring back a skin of ale."

"Friend, thou hast said enough," said the beggar, getting down from the stile. "I will feast thee with the best I have."

So Robin straightway left the beggar, who, upon his part, went to a budding lime bush back of the hedge, and there spread his feast upon the grass and roasted his eggs upon a little fagot fire with a deftness gained by long labor in that line. After a while back came Robin bearing a skin of ale upon his shoulder. Then the one seized upon the ale and the other upon the pie, and nothing was heard for a while but the munching of food and the gurgle of ale as it left the skin.

At last, Robin pushed the food from him and heaved a sigh of deep content. "And now, good friend," quoth he, leaning upon one elbow, "I would have at thee about the other serious matter of which I spoke. I have taken a liking to thy craft and would fain have a taste of a beggar's life. Methinks I shall change clothes with thee, and I will give thee two golden angels to boot. I have brought my staff, thinking that I might have to rap someone of the brethren of thy cloth over the head by way of argument in this matter, but I love thee so much for the feast thou hast given me that I would not lift even my little finger against thee."

"Lift thy finger against me, forsooth! Art thou out of thy wits?" cried the beggar, rising and taking up his staff. "My name is Riccon Hazel, and I come from Flintshire. I have cracked the head of many a better man than thou. Thou shalt not have so much as one tagrag of my coat. So take up thy club and defend thyself."

Then up leaped merry Robin and snatched up his staff also; and, ere you could count three, Riccon's staff was over the hedge, and Riccon himself lay upon the grass. Then Robin, seeing that he was stunned with the blow, brought the skin of ale and poured some of it on the beggar's head and some down his throat, so that presently he opened his eyes and looked around.

"Now, good fellow," Robin said, "wilt thou change clothes with me, or shall I tap thee again?"

Then Riccon sat up and rubbed the bump on his crown. "If I must give up my clothes, I must," quoth he. "But first promise me that thou wilt take naught from me but my clothes."

"I promise on the word of a true yeoman," quoth Robin.

Thereupon the beggar drew a little knife and, ripping up the lining of his coat, took thence ten golden pounds, which he laid beside him with a wink at Robin. "Now thou may'st have my clothes and welcome," said he, "and thou mightest have had them without the cost of a farthing, far less two golden angels."

"Marry," quoth Robin, laughing, "thou art a sly fellow. Had I known thou hadst so much thou might'st not have carried it away, for I warrant thou didst not come honestly by it."

Then each put on the other's clothes, and as lusty a beggar was Robin Hood as e'er you could find. But Riccon skipped and danced for joy of the fair suit of Lincoln green. Quoth he, "Thou may'st keep the cold pieces of the feast, friend, for I mean to live well while my money lasts and my clothes are gay."

So he left Robin and, crossing the stile, was gone. Then Robin strolled onward until he came to where a little grass-grown path left the road and, for no reason but that his fancy led him, he took the path and so came to a little dingle, where four lusty fellows sat with legs outstretched around a goodly feast.

Four merry beggars were they, and each had slung about his neck a little board that rested upon his breast. One board had written upon it, *I Am Blind*, another, *I Am Deaf*, another, *I Am Dumb*, and the fourth, *Pity the Lame One*.

The deaf man was the first to hear Robin, for he said, "Hark, brothers, I hear someone coming." And the blind man was the first to see him, for he said, "He is an honest man, and one of like craft to ourselves." Then the dumb man called to him in a great voice, "Welcome, brother; come and sit while there is still a little malmsey in the bottle." At this, the lame man, who had taken off his wooden leg and unstrapped his own leg, and was sitting with it stretched out upon the grass so as to rest it, made room for Robin and held out the flask of malmsey.

"Marry," quoth Robin, laughing, "methinks it is no more than seemly of you all to be glad to see me, seeing that I bring sight to the blind, speech to the dumb, hearing to the deaf, and a lusty leg to a lame man. I drink to your happiness, as I may not drink to your health, seeing ye are already hale."

At this all grinned, and the blind beggar smote Robin upon the shoulder, swearing he was a right merry wag.

"Whence comest thou, lad?" asked the dumb man.

"Why," quoth Robin, "I came this morning from sleeping overnight in Sherwood."

"Is it even so?" said the deaf man. "I would not for all the money we are carrying sleep one night in Sherwood. If Robin Hood caught one of our trade in his woodlands he would, methinks, clip his ears."

"Methinks he would, too," quoth Robin, laughing. "But what money is that that ye speak of?"

Then up spoke the lame man. "Our king, Peter of York," said he, "hath sent us to Lincoln with those moneys that—"

"Stay," quoth the blind man, "I would not doubt our brother

here, but bear in mind we know him not. What art thou, brother? Upright-man, Jurk-man, Clapper-dudgeon or Abraham-man?"

At these words Robin looked from one man to the other with mouth agape. "Truly," quoth he, "I am an upright man, at least, I strive to be; but I know not what thou meanest by such jargon."

A silence fell on all. "Thou dost surely jest when thou sayest that thou dost not understand," quoth the blind man. "Answer me this: Hast thou ever fibbed a chouse quarrons in the Rome pad?"

"Now out upon it," quoth Robin Hood testily. "Ye make sport of me by pattering such gibberish. I have the best part of a mind to crack your heads, and would do so, too, but for the sweet malmsey ye have given me."

But the four beggars leaped to their feet and snatched up their cudgels. Then Robin, albeit he knew not what the coil was about, leaped to his feet also and clapped his back against a tree. "How, now!" cried he, twirling his staff betwixt his fingers. "Would you four fellows set upon one man? Stand back, or I will score your pates till they have as many marks upon them as a pothouse door! Are ye mad? I have done you no harm."

"Thou liest!" quoth the one who pretended to be blind. "Thou hast come as a spy. But thine ears have heard too much for thy body's good, and this day thou shalt die!" Then, whirling up his cudgel, he rushed upon Robin. But Robin struck two blows as quick as a wink, and down went the blind man on the grass.

At this the others bore back and stood at a little distance scowling upon Robin. Then, seeing them so hesitate, Robin leaped upon them, striking even as he leaped. Down went the dumb man, and away flew his cudgel as he fell. At this the others took to their heels as though they had the west wind's boots upon their feet. Robin looked after them, laughing, and thought that never had he seen so fleet a runner as the lame man.

Then Robin turned to the two upon the ground. Quoth he, "These fellows spoke somewhat about certain moneys; methinks it were a pity to let sound money stay in the pockets of such thieving knaves." So saying, he stooped over the blind man and searched among his rags, till presently his fingers felt a leathern pouch. In it were four round rolls wrapped up in sheepskin; and in each one Robin found fifty bright new-stamped golden pounds. His mouth gaped. Quoth he, "I have oft heard that the Beggars' Guild was overrich, but never did I think they sent such sums as this to their treasury. I shall take it with me, for it will be better used for charity." So saying, he thrust the pouch into his own bosom. Then taking up his staff, he went merrily on his way.

He strode along, singing as he went; and so blithe was he and so fresh and clean, that every lass he met had a sweet word for him, while the dogs, that most times hate a beggar, wagged their tails; for dogs know an honest man by his smell, and honest Robin was— in his own way. Thus he went till he came to the wayside cross nigh Ollerton. Being somewhat tired, he sat him down upon the grassy bank, and after a time he saw someone drawing near, riding upon a horse. The traveler was a thin, wizened man, and, to look upon him, you could not tell whether he was thirty years old or sixty. As for the nag, it was as thin as the rider.

Robin laughed at the droll sight, but he knew the wayfarer to be a certain rich corn engrosser, who more than once had bought all the grain in the countryside and held it till it reached famine prices, thus making much money from poor people's needs.

So, after a while, the corn engrosser came riding up to where Robin sat; whereupon Robin stepped forth and laid his hand upon the horse's rein, calling upon the other to stop.

"Now, out upon thee!" snarled the other. "Such rogues as thou art are better dancing upon nothing, with a hempen collar about the neck, than strolling the highways so freely."

Then Robin looked up and down, as if to see that no one was nigh, and coming close to the corn engrosser stood on tiptoe and spoke in his ear. "Thinkest thou insooth that I am as I seem to be? Look upon me. There is not a grain of dirt upon my hands or face. Didst thou ever see a beggar so? Look, friend." Here he took the purse from his breast and showed to the dazzled eyes of the corn engrosser the bright golden pieces. "These rags but hide an honest rich man from the eyes of Robin Hood."

"Put up thy money, lad," cried the other quickly. "Art thou a fool, to trust to beggar's rags to shield thee from Robin Hood? If he caught thee, he would strip thee to the skin, for he hates a lusty beggar as he doth a fat priest or those of my kind."

"Is it indeed so?" quoth Robin. "Had I known this, I had not come in this garb. But I must go forward now, as much depends upon my journeying! Where goest thou, friend?"

"I go to Newark," said the corn engrosser.

"Why, I myself am on the way to Newark," quoth Robin, "so that, as two honest men are better than one in roads beset by such as this Robin Hood, I will jog along with thee."

"Why, as thou art an honest fellow and a rich fellow," said the corn engrosser, "I mind not thy company."

"Then forward," quoth Robin, "for the day wanes and it will be dark ere we reach Newark." So off they went, the lean horse hobbling along as before, and Robin pacing beside.

So they traveled along till they reached a hill on the outskirts of Sherwood. Here the lean man turned in his saddle and spoke to Robin for the first time since they had left the cross. "Here is thy greatest danger, friend," said he, "for here we are nighest to where that vile thief dwells."

"Alas!" quoth Robin, "I would that I had as little money by me as thou hast, for I fear this Robin Hood."

Then the other winked cunningly at Robin. Quoth he, "I tell thee, friend, I have nigh as much as thou hast, but it is hidden. See thou these clogs upon my feet?"

"Yea, truly, they are large enough for any man to see."

"The soles are not what they seem to be," said the corn engrosser. "Each is a little box, and the upper of the shoe lifts up like a lid, and within each shoe are fourscore and ten bright golden pounds, all wrapped in hair to keep them from telling tales of themselves."

When the corn engrosser had told this, Robin broke into a roar of laughter and stopped the sad-looking nag. "Stay, good friend," quoth he, "on second thoughts I go no farther. Thou may go forward if thou list, but thou must go forward barefoot, for I have taken a great fancy to thy shoon."

At these words the corn factor grew pale as a linen napkin. "Who art thou that talkest so?" said he.

Then Robin laughed, and quoth he, "Men hereabout call me Robin Hood; so thou hadst best do my bidding, and hasten, I prithee, or thou wilt not get to Newark Town till after dark."

At the sound of the name of Robin Hood, the corn factor quaked with fear, so that he had to seize his horse by the mane to save himself from falling off its back. Then, without more words, he stripped off his clogs and let them fall upon the road. Then Robin said, "Take a fool's advice of me, sweet friend, and come no more so nigh to Sherwood, or mayhap someday thou may'st of a sudden find a cloth-yard shaft betwixt thy ribs." Hereupon he clapped his hand to the horse's flank and off went nag and rider.

When he was fairly gone, Robin turned, laughing, and entered the forest carrying the shoes in his hand.

That night in Sherwood the fires glowed brightly, and all around sat the stout fellows of the band to hear Robin Hood and Little John tell their adventures. When all was told, Friar Tuck spoke up. "Good master, thou hast had a pretty time, but still I hold that the life of the barefoot friar is the merrier of the two."

"Nay," quoth Will Stutely, "I hold with our master, that he hath had the pleasanter doings of the two, for he hath had two stout bouts at quarterstaff this day."

So some of the band held with Robin Hood and some with Little John. As for me, I think— But I leave it with you to say for yourselves which you hold with.

Robin Hood Shoots Before Queen Eleanor

THE HIGHROAD STRETCHED white and dusty in the hot summer afternoon sun, and the trees stood motionless along the roadside. All across the meadowlands the hot air quivered, and in the limpid waters of the lowland brook the fish hung motionless above the yellow gravel.

Along the road a youth came riding upon a milk-white barb, and folk stopped and looked after him, for never had so lovely a lad been seen in Nottingham before. He could not have been more than sixteen years of age. His long yellow hair flowed behind him, and he was clad in silk and velvet, his dagger jingling against the pommel of the saddle. Thus came the Queen's Page, young Richard Partington, from famous London Town to Sherwood Forest.

His journey had been long, and young Partington was right glad when he saw before him a little inn with a sign bearing the picture of a blue boar. Five lusty fellows sat drinking beer upon a bench, two of the stoutest clothed in Lincoln green.

Here the fair lad drew rein and called loudly for Rhenish wine, for stout country ale was too coarse a drink for this young gentleman. The landlord brought a bottle of wine and a long narrow glass upon a salver, which he held up to the page as he sat upon his horse. Young Partington poured forth the bright yellow wine, and holding the glass aloft cried, "Here is to the health and happiness of the noble Queen Eleanor; may my journey and her desirings soon have end, and I find a certain stout yeoman men call Robin Hood."

At these words, the two in Lincoln green began whispering. Then one of the two, whom Partington thought to be the tallest fellow he had ever beheld, spoke up: "What does our good Queen Eleanor wish of Robin Hood, Sir Page? Methinks I and my friend here might safely guide thee to him. Yet I tell thee plainly, we would not for all merry England have aught of harm befall him."

"Set thy mind at ease; I bring naught of ill," quoth Partington. "I bring a kind message to him from our Queen."

Then the tall yeoman said, "Surely it were safe, Will"; whereat the other nodded. Thereupon Partington paid his score, and, the yeomen coming forward, they all departed on their way.

Robin Hood and many of his band were lying upon the grass under the greenwood tree when Little John and Will Stutely came into the open glade, young Richard Partington riding between them. Then Robin arose and stepped forth to meet him, and Partington leaped from his horse and doffed his cap.

"Now, welcome fair youth!" cried Robin. "And tell me, I

prithee, what bringeth one clad in such noble garb to our forest?"

Then young Partington said, "If I err not, thou art the famous outlaw Robin Hood. To thee I bring greetings from our noble Queen Eleanor. Oft hath she heard thee spoken of, and fain would she behold thy face; therefore she bids me tell thee that if thou wilt presently come to London Town, she will do all in her power to guard thee against harm, and will send thee back safe to Sherwood. Four days hence, in Finsbury Fields, our good King Henry holdeth a grand shooting match, and all the most famous archers of England will be there. Our Queen would fain see thee strive with these, knowing that if thou come thou wilt, with little doubt, carry off the prize. She sends thee, as a sign of great goodwill, this golden ring, which I give herewith into thy hands."

Then Robin Hood kissed the ring and slipped it upon his little finger. Quoth he, "Ere this ring departs from me, my hand shall be cold in death. Sir Page, I will do our Queen's bidding."

"If there be any of thy band that thou wouldst take with thee," said the page, "our Queen will make them right welcome."

"I will choose three," quoth Robin, "and these three shall be Little John, Will Scarlet and Allan a Dale. Thou, Will Stutely, shall be the chief of the band while I am gone."

Then they prepared themselves for the journey, and a right fair sight they made, for Robin was clad in all blue, and Little John and Will Scarlet in good Lincoln green, and Allan a Dale was dressed in scarlet from the crown of his head to the toes of his pointed shoes. Each wore beneath his cap a little head covering of burnished steel, and underneath his jerkin a coat of linked mail as fine as carded wool, yet so tough that no arrow could pierce it. Then young Partington mounted his horse again, and the five departed. For four days they traveled, and on the fifth morning they came at last to the towers and walls of London Town.

Queen Eleanor sat in her bower, and about her stood her ladies-in-waiting chatting in low voices. She herself sat dreamily where the air came drifting into the room laden with the perfumes of the roses that bloomed in the royal garden. To her came one who said that Partington and four yeomen waited her pleasure in the court below. Then Queen Eleanor arose joyously and bade them be shown into her presence.

Thus Robin Hood and Little John and Will Scarlet and Allan a Dale came before the Queen. Robin knelt before her with his hands folded upon his breast, saying, "Here am I, Robin Hood. Lo, I am thy true servant, and will do thy bidding, even if it be to the shedding of the last drop of my life's blood."

Good Queen Eleanor smiled pleasantly upon him; then she made them all be seated to rest. Rich food was brought and noble wines, and after they had eaten, she questioned them of their adventures. They told her all of the lusty doings herein spoken of, and among others that concerning Sir Richard of the Lea, and how the Bishop had abided three days in Sherwood Forest. At this, the Queen and her ladies laughed again and again; and the time passed till the hour drew nigh for the great archery match.

A gay sight were famous Finsbury Fields on that sunny morning. The King's yeomen were divided into ten companies of fourscore men, and each company had a captain over it. Along the end of the meadow stood booths of striped canvas, one for each band, and at the peak of each fluttered a flag. From the center booth hung the yellow flag of Tepus, the famous bow bearer of the King; next to it, on one hand, was the blue flag of Gilbert of the White Hand, and on the other the blood-red pennant of young Clifton of Buckinghamshire; for these were the most famous of all. On each side of the range were rows upon rows of seats, and in the center of the north side was a raised dais for the King and Queen. All the benches were full of people, rising head above head high aloft till it made the eye dizzy to look upon them.

At last a blast of bugles sounded, and into the meadow came riding six trumpeters with silver trumpets, from which hung velvet banners heavy with rich workings of silver and gold thread. Behind these came King Henry upon a dapple-gray stallion, with his Queen beside him upon a milk-white palfrey. On either side of them walked the yeomen of the guard, the sunlight flashing on their steel halberds. Then came the court in a great crowd, so that all the lawn was alive with waving plumes and flashing jewels.

Then all the people arose and shouted, so that their voices sounded like the storm upon the Cornish coast, when the dark waves run upon the shore and leap and break amid the rocks; so the King and Queen came to their place, and there were seated on thrones bedecked with purple silks and cloths of silver and of gold.

When all was quiet a bugle sounded, and straightway forty-score stalwart archers came marching in order from their tents and stood in front of King Henry. The King looked up and down their ranks right proudly; then his herald, Sir Hugh de Mowbray, proclaimed the rules governing the game, and that the first prize was to be twoscore and ten golden pounds, a silver bugle horn inlaid with gold, and a quiver with ten white arrows tipped with gold and feathered with the white swan's wing. The second prize was to be fivescore of the finest harts that run on Dallen Lea, to be shot when the yeoman that won them chose. The third prize was to be two tuns of good Rhenish wine.

When Sir Hugh had done, each band marched in order back to its place. And now the shooting began, the captains first taking stand, each speeding seven shafts and then making room for the men who shot, each in turn, after them. When the shooting was done each target looked like the back of a hedgehog when the farm dog snuffs at it. Then the judges came forward, looked carefully at the targets, and proclaimed which three had shot the best in each band. Then ten fresh targets were brought forward, and these archers took their places once more.

This time three shafts were shot by each archer. Then the judges again called aloud the best bowman of each band. Of these Gilbert of the White Hand led, for six of the ten arrows he had shot had lodged in the center; but stout Tepus and young Clifton trod close upon his heels. And now those fellows that were left went back to their tents to rest and change their bowstrings.

Then while a deep buzz of talking sounded all around, the King turned to Queen Eleanor, and quoth he, "Truly these yeomen are the very best archers in all the wide world."

"Yet," said the Queen, "I know of three yeomen that I would not fear to match against the best three from among thy guard,

and, moreover, I will match them here this day, but only providing thou wilt grant a free pardon to all that come in my behalf."

The King laughed loud and long. "Truly," said he, "thou art
taking up with strange matters for a queen. If thou wilt bring those
three I promise to give them free pardon for forty days. Moreover,
if they shoot better than my yeomen, man for man, they shall have
the prizes for themselves. But as thou hast so taken up with sports,
hast thou a mind for a wager?"

"Why, insooth," said Queen Eleanor. "I know naught of such
matters, but I will strive to pleasure thee. What wilt thou wager?"

Then the King laughed again, for he loved a goodly jest. "I
will wager thee ten tuns of the stoutest ale," he said, "and tenscore
bows of tempered Spanish yew, with quivers and arrows to match."

All that stood around smiled at this, for it seemed a merry
wager for a king to give to a queen; but Queen Eleanor said
quietly, "I will take thy wager, for I know right well where to
place those things. Now, who will be on my side in this matter?
Wilt thou, my Lord Bishop of Hereford?"

"Nay," quoth the Bishop, who sat nearby, "it ill befits one of
my cloth to deal in such matters. Moreover, there are no such archers as his Majesty's in all the world; I would but lose my money."

"Methinks the thought of thy gold weigheth more heavily with
thee than the wrong to thy cloth," said the Queen, smiling. Then
she turned to a knight who stood near, whose name was Sir Robert Lee. "Wilt thou back me?" said she. "Thou art surely rich
enough to risk so much for the sake of a lady."

"To pleasure my Queen I will do it," said Sir Robert, "but for
the sake of no other in all the world would I wager a groat, for
no man can stand against Tepus and Gilbert and Clifton."

Then Queen Eleanor said to the King, "I want no such aid as
Sir Robert giveth me; but against thy beer and bows I wager this
girdle all set with jewels from around my waist; and surely that
is worth more than thine."

"Now, I take thy wager," quoth the King. "Send for thine
archers. But here come forth the others; let them shoot, and then
I will match those that win against all the world."

"So be it," said the Queen. Thereupon, beckoning to Richard Partington, she whispered something in his ear, and the page bowed and crossed the meadow to the other side of the range, where he was lost in the crowd. At this, all that stood around whispered to one another, wondering what it meant.

And now the ten archers of the King's guard took their stand again. Carefully each man shot three shafts, and so deep was the silence of the crowd that you could hear every arrow rap against the target. Then, when the last shaft had sped, a great roar went up. Once again Gilbert had lodged three arrows in the white; Tepus came second with two in the white and one in the black ring next to it; but stout Clifton had gone down and Hubert of Suffolk had taken the third place.

All the archers around Gilbert's booth shouted for joy, tossing their caps aloft, and shaking hands with one another.

In the midst of all the hubbub four strangers came across the lawn toward the King's pavilion. The first was a yeoman clad in blue, and behind came two in Lincoln green and one in scarlet. This last carried three stout bows of yew, inlaid with silver and gold. And all the folk leaned forward to see what was toward.

When they came before the King and Queen, the four yeomen bent their knees and doffed their caps. King Henry leaned far forward and stared at them closely, but the Bishop of Hereford started as though stung by a wasp.

Then the Queen leaned forward and spoke in a clear voice. "Locksley," said she, "I have made a wager with the King that thou and two of thy men can outshoot any three that he can send against you. Wilt thou do thy best for my sake?"

"Yea," quoth Robin Hood, to whom she spoke, "and, if I fail, I make my vow never to finger bowstring more."

Now, although Little John had been somewhat abashed in the Queen's bower, when the soles of his feet pressed green grass he felt himself again; so he said boldly, "Now, blessings on thy sweet face. An there lived a man that would not do his best for thee—I would like to have the cracking of his knave's pate!"

"Peace, Little John!" said Robin Hood hastily, in a low voice;

but good Queen Eleanor laughed aloud, and a ripple of merriment sounded all over the booth.

The Bishop of Hereford did not laugh; neither did the King, but he turned to the Queen, and quoth he, "Who are these men?"

Then up spoke the Bishop hastily, for he could hold his peace no longer: "Your Majesty, yon fellow in blue is a certain outlawed thief of the mid-country named Robin Hood; yon tall, strapping villain goeth by the name of Little John; the other in green is a certain backsliding gentleman known as Will Scarlet; the man in red is a rogue of a northern minstrel named Allan a Dale."

At this speech the King's brows drew together blackly, and he turned to the Queen. "Is this true?" said he sternly.

"Yea," said the Queen, smiling, "and truly the Bishop should know them well, for he spent three days in merry sport with Robin Hood in Sherwood Forest. But bear in mind that thou hast promised the safety of these good yeomen for forty days."

"I will keep my promise," said the King, in a deep voice that showed his anger, "but when these forty days are gone let this outlaw look to himself." Then he turned to Gilbert, Tepus and Hubert, who stood nearby. Quoth he, "I have pledged myself that ye shall shoot against three of these knaves. If ye outshoot them I will fill your caps with silver pennies; if ye fail ye shall lose your prizes that ye have won so fairly. Do your best, lads, and if ye win ye shall be glad of it to the last of your life."

Then the archers of the King went and told their friends all that had passed; and from the archers the news was taken up by the crowd, so that at last everybody stood up, craning their necks to catch sight of the famous outlaws.

Six fresh targets were now set up, one for each man; whereupon Robin Hood and Gilbert of the White Hand tossed a farthing aloft to see who should lead in the shooting, and the lot fell to Gilbert's side; thereupon he called upon Hubert of Suffolk to lead.

Hubert took his place, planted his foot firmly, and fitted an arrow; then, breathing upon his fingertips, he drew the string slowly and carefully. The arrow sped true, and lodged in the white; again he shot, and again he hit the clout; a third shaft he sped, but this time failed of the center, and but struck the black, yet not more than a finger's breadth from the white.

Then Will Scarlet took his place; but, because of overcaution, he spoiled his target with the very first arrow that he sped, for he hit the next ring to the black, the second from the center. "Lad, lad," quoth Robin, "hold not the string so long! Have I not often told thee overcaution spilleth the milk?" To this Will Scarlet took heed, so the next arrows he shot lodged fairly in the center ring; but, for all that, Hubert had outshot him. Then all that looked on shouted with joy, because Hubert had overcome the stranger.

Quoth the King grimly to the Queen, "If thine archers shoot no better than that, thou art like to lose thy wager, lady." But Queen Eleanor smiled, for she looked for better things from Robin Hood and Little John.

Now Tepus took his place. The first arrow struck the center ring, but then he, also, took overheed, and the second smote the black; the last arrow was tipped with luck, for it smote the very center of the clout. Quoth Robin, "That is the sweetest shot that hath been sped this day; but, nevertheless, friend Tepus, thy cake is burned, methinks. Little John, it is thy turn next."

Little John shot his three arrows quickly; yet all three smote the center. But at this no shouting was heard, for the folk of London Town did not like to see stout Tepus overcome by a fellow from the countryside.

And now stout Gilbert took his place and shot with the greatest care; and again he struck all three shafts into the clout.

"Well done, Gilbert!" quoth Robin, smiting him upon the shoulder. "I make my vow, thou art one of the best archers that ever mine eyes beheld."

Then the King muttered in his beard, "Now, blessed Saint Hubert, if thou wilt but jog that rogue's elbow, I will give eight-score waxen candles to thy chapel nigh Matching." But it may be Saint Hubert's ears were stuffed with tow, for he seemed not to hear the King's prayer this day.

Having gotten three shafts to his liking, Robin looked carefully to his bowstring ere he shot. "Yea," quoth he to Gilbert, who stood nigh him to watch his shooting, "thou shouldst pay us a visit at merry Sherwood." Here he drew the bowstring to his ear. "In London"—here he loosed his shaft—"thou canst find naught to shoot at but rooks and daws; there one can tickle the ribs of the noblest stags in England." So he shot even while he talked, yet the shaft lodged not more than half an inch from the very center.

"By my soul!" cried Gilbert. "Art thou the devil in blue, to shoot in that wise?"

"Nay," quoth Robin, laughing, "not quite so ill as that, I trust." And again he shot, and again he smote his arrow close beside the center; a third time he dropped his arrow betwixt the other two and into the very center, so that the feathers of all three were ruffled together, seeming from a distance to be one thick shaft.

And now a low murmur ran among the crowd, for never before had London seen such shooting as this. Stout Gilbert clapped his palm to Robin's, owning that he could never hope to draw such a bowstring as Robin Hood. But the King was full of wrath. "Nay!" cried he, clenching his hands upon the arms of his seat. "Gilbert is not yet beaten! Did he not strike the clout thrice? Go thou, Sir Hugh, and bid them shoot another round, and another, till either he or that knave Robin Hood is overcome." Then Sir Hugh went straightway and told them what the King had said.

So Gilbert took his place once more, but this time he failed, for, a sudden little wind arising, his shaft missed the center ring, but by not more than the breadth of a barley straw.

"Thine eggs are cracked, Gilbert," quoth Robin, laughing; and once more he smote the white circle of the center.

Then the King arose; not a word said he, but looked around with a baleful look. Then he and his Queen and all the court left the place, but the King's heart was brimming full of wrath.

After the King had gone, all the yeomen of the archer guard came crowding around Robin, and Little John, and Will, and Allan, to snatch a look at these famous fellows from the mid-country; and with them came many onlookers.

Then the chief judge came forward and said to Robin, "The first prize belongeth rightly to thee; so here I give thee the silver bugle, here the quiver of arrows, and here a purse of twoscore and ten golden pounds." And he handed those things to Robin. Then he said to Little John, "To thee belongeth the second prize, to wit, fivescore of the finest harts that run on Dallen Lea. Thou mayest shoot them whensoever thou dost list." Last of all he said to stout Hubert, "Thou hast held thine own, and so thou hast kept the prize duly thine, to wit, two tuns of good Rhenish wine. These shall be delivered to thee whensoever thou dost list."

Then up spoke Robin: "This silver bugle I keep in honor of this shooting match; but thou, Gilbert, art the best archer of all the King's guard, and to thee I freely give this purse of gold. Would it were ten times as much, for thou art a right yeoman, good and true. To each of the ten that last shot I give one of these golden shafts. Keep them always by you, so that ye may tell your grandchildren that ye are the stoutest yeomen in all the world." At this all shouted aloud, for it pleased them to hear Robin speak so.

Then up spoke Little John. "Good friend Tepus," said he, "I want not those harts of Dallen Lea, for we have more than enow in our own country. Twoscore and ten I give to thee for thine own shooting, and five I give to each band for their pleasure."

At this many tossed their caps aloft, and swore that no better fellows ever walked the sod than Robin Hood and his yeomen.

Then a burly yeoman of the King's guard came forward and plucked Robin by the sleeve. "Good master," quoth he, "a young peacock of a page, one Richard Partington, was seeking thee without avail in the crowd, and told me that he bore a message to thee from a certain lady that thou wottest of. This message he bade me tell thee privily. Let me see—I trust I have forgot it not—yea, thus it was: 'The lion growls. Beware thy head.'"

"Is it so?" quoth Robin, starting, for he knew right well that it was the Queen sent the message, and that she spoke of the King's wrath. "Now, I thank thee, good fellow, for thou hast done me greater service than thou knowest of this day." Then he called his three yeomen together and told them privately that they had best be jogging. So, without tarrying, they made their way through the crowd; then they left London Town and started northward.

Now it happened that after the King left the archery ground, he went straightway to his cabinet, and with him went the Bishop and Sir Robert Lee; but the King said never a word, but sat gnawing his lip, for his heart was galled within him. At last the Bishop spoke, in a sorrowful voice: "It is a sad thing, your Majesty, that this knavish outlaw should be let escape; for, let him but get back to Sherwood, and he may snap his fingers at king and king's men."

"Say'st thou so?" quoth the King grimly. "Nay, when the forty days are past, I will seize upon this thieving outlaw, if I have to tear down all of Sherwood to find him."

Then the Bishop spoke again, in his soft, smooth voice: "Forgive my boldness, your Majesty, and believe that I have naught but the good of England at heart; but what would it boot though my gracious lord did root up every tree of Sherwood? There are many other woodlands in Nottingham and Derby, Lincoln and York, amid any of which your Majesty might as well think to seize upon Robin Hood as to lay finger upon a rat among the dust and broken things of a garret. Nay, if he doth once plant foot in the woodland, he is lost to the law forever."

The King tapped his fingertips upon the table beside him with vexation. "What wouldst thou have me do, Bishop?" quoth he. "Didst thou not hear me pledge my word to the Queen?"

"Far be it from me," said the cunning Bishop, "to point the way to one so clear-sighted as your Majesty; but, were I the King of England, I should look upon the matter in this wise. Suppose I had promised to do her Majesty's bidding, whereupon she bade me to slay myself; should I, then, run blindly upon my sword? I would say unto myself, A woman knoweth naught of state government; and, likewise, a woman is ever prone to take up a fancy, even as she would pluck a daisy from the roadside and then throw it away when the savor is gone; therefore, though she hath taken a fancy to this outlaw, it will soon be forgotten. As for me, am I to let the greatest villain in England slip from my grasp?" So the Bishop talked, and the King lent his ear to his evil counsel, until, after a while, he turned to Sir Robert Lee and bade him send six yeomen of the guard to take Robin and his three men prisoners.

Now Sir Robert Lee was a gentle knight, and he felt grieved to see the King so break his promise; nevertheless, he said nothing, for he saw how bitterly the King was set against Robin Hood; but he did not send the yeomen of the guard at once; he went first to the Queen, and bade her send word to Robin of his danger. This he did, not for the well-being of Robin, but because he would save his lord's honor. Thus it came about that when the yeomen of the guard went to the archery field, they found not Robin.

The afternoon was well-nigh gone when Robin Hood, Little John, Will and Allan set forth upon their homeward way, and the great round moon was floating in the eastern sky when they saw before them the twinkling lights of Barnet Town, some twelve miles from London. Down they walked through the stony streets and past the cozy houses, and so came at last to a little inn. The spot pleased Robin well, and he said, "Here will we rest, for we are well away from London Town and our King's wrath."

"I could wish that we were farther, Uncle," quoth Will Scarlet. "Nevertheless, if thou thinkest best, let us in for the night."

So in they went and called for the best that the place afforded. But when they were done eating, the landlord came in of a sudden, and said that there was at the door a certain Richard Partington, who wished to speak with the lad in blue.

So Robin arose quickly, and found young Richard sitting upon his horse in the moonlight. "What news bearest thou, Sir Page?" said Robin. "I trust that it is not of an ill nature."

"Why," said young Partington, "it is ill enow. The King hath been bitterly stirred up against thee by that vile Bishop of Hereford. Not finding thee at Finsbury Fields, he hath gathered together fiftyscore and more armed men, and is sending them in haste along this very road, to prevent thy getting back to Sherwood. He hath given the Bishop command over all these men, and thou knowest what thou hast to expect of him—short shrift and a long rope. So thou hadst best get thee gone from this place. This word the Queen hath bidden me bring to thee."

"Now, Richard Partington," quoth Robin, "I thank thee. Thou may'st tell the good Queen that I will leave this place without delay, and will let the landlord think that we are going to Saint Albans; but when we are upon the highroad again, I will go one way to Sherwood and will send my men the other, so that if one falleth into the King's hands the others may haply escape. And now, Sir Page, I wish thee farewell."

"Farewell, thou bold yeoman," said young Partington, "and may'st thou reach thy hiding in safety."

So each shook the other's hand, and the lad turned back toward London, while Robin entered the inn once more. There he found his yeomen waiting his coming; likewise the landlord was there, for he was curious to know what Master Partington had to do with the fellow in blue. "Up, my merry men!" quoth Robin. "There are those after us with whom we will stand but an ill chance. So we will go forward to Saint Albans." Hereupon he paid the landlord his score, and so they left the inn.

When they had come without the town, Robin told them all that had passed. Then he told them that they three should go to the eastward and he would go to the westward, and so, skirting the main highroads, they would come by devious paths to Sherwood. Then Robin kissed the three upon the cheeks, and so they parted.

Not long after this, a score of the King's men came clattering up to the inn at Barnet Town. They leaped from their horses and surrounded the place, but found that the birds had flown.

"Methought that they were naughty fellows," said the host. "But I heard that blue-clad knave say they would go to Saint Albans; so, an ye hurry, ye may catch them betwixt here and there." At this the band set forth again, galloping toward Saint Albans.

Little John and Will Scarlet and Allan a Dale traveled eastward, until they came to Chelmsford, in Essex. Thence they turned northward, and came through Cambridge and Lincolnshire, to the good town of Gainsborough. Then, striking to the westward and the south, they came at last to the northern borders of Sherwood.

Eight days they journeyed thus; but when they got to the green-wood glade they found that Robin had not yet returned.

For Robin was not as lucky as his men had been. Having left the great north road and turned his face to the west, he came to Woodstock, in Oxfordshire. Thence he traveled northward, till he came to Dudley, in Staffordshire. Seven days it took him to journey thus far, and then, turning toward the eastward, shunning the main roads, he went by way of Litchfield until he came to a place called Stanton. Now Robin thought that his danger had gone by; but there is many a slip betwixt the cup and the lip, and this Robin was to find. For thus it was:

When the King's men found themselves foiled at Saint Albans, they knew not what to do. Presently another band of horsemen came, and another, until all the moonlit streets were full of armed men. Betwixt midnight and dawn came the Bishop of Hereford also. He gathered his bands together and pushed northward with speed. On the evening of the fourth day he reached Nottingham Town, and there divided his men into bands of six or seven, and sent them all through the countryside, blocking every highway and byway to the eastward and the southward and the westward of Sherwood. The Sheriff of Nottingham called forth all his men likewise, for he saw that this was the best chance that had ever befallen of paying back his score to Robin Hood.

But of all this Robin knew not a whit; so he whistled merrily as he trudged along the road beyond Stanton. At last he came to where a little stream spread across the road in a shallow sheet, tinkling and sparkling as it fretted over its bed of golden gravel. Here Robin stopped and, kneeling down, he made a cup of the palms of his hands, and began to drink. On either side of the road stood tangled thickets, and it pleased Robin's heart to hear the little birds singing therein. But of a sudden a gray goose shaft hissed past his ear, and struck with a splash into the water beside him. Robin sprang to his feet, and, at one bound, crossed the stream and the roadside and plunged headlong into the thicket. Then up the road came riding some of the King's men at headlong speed. They leaped from their horses and plunged into the thicket after Robin. But Robin, crawling here, stooping there and running across some little open, soon left them far behind, coming out upon another road about eight hundred paces distant. For a moment he stood listening to the shouts of the men as they beat in the thickets like hounds that had lost the scent of their quarry. Then, buckling his belt more tightly, he ran fleetly down the road toward Sherwood.

But Robin had not gone more than three furlongs when he came to the brow of a hill, and saw another band of the King's men in the valley beneath him. Seeing that they had not caught sight of him, he turned back, knowing that it was better to run the chance of escaping those fellows that were yet in the thickets than to rush into the arms of those in the valley. He ran with all speed, and had gotten safely past the thickets, when the seven men came forth into the open road. They raised a great shout when they saw him, but Robin was then a quarter of a mile and more away from them, coursing over the ground like a greyhound. He never slackened his pace till he had come nigh to Mackworth, over beyond the Derwent River. Here, seeing that he was out of present danger, he sat down beneath a hedge to catch his wind.

Now along that road came plodding a certain cobbler, one Quince, of Derby, who had been to take a pair of shoes to a farmer nigh Kirk Langly. Good Quince was an honest fellow, but his wits were somewhat of the heavy sort, like unbaked dough, so that the only thing that was in his mind was, Three shillings sixpence ha'penny for thy shoon; and this traveled round and round inside of his head, as a pea in an empty pot.

"Halloa, good friend," quoth Robin, from beneath the hedge, when the other had gotten nigh. "Whither away so merrily?"

The cobbler stopped, and, seeing a well-clad stranger in blue, he spoke to him in seemly wise. "Give ye good den, fair sir, and I would say that I come from Kirk Langly, where I ha' sold my shoon for three shillings sixpence ha'penny. But, an I may be so bold, what dost thou there beneath the hedge?"

"Marry," quoth merry Robin, "I sit beneath the hedge here to drop salt on the tails of golden birds."

At these words the cobbler's eyes opened big and wide with

wonder. "Alackaday," quoth he, "I ha' never seen those same golden birds. And dost thou insooth find them in these hedges?"

"Aye, truly," quoth Robin, "they are as thick here as fresh herring in Cannock Chase."

"And dost thou insooth catch them by dropping salt on their pretty tails?" said the cobbler, all drowned in wonder.

"Yea," quoth Robin, "but this salt is of an odd kind, for it can only be gotten by boiling down a quart of moonbeams, and then one hath but a pinch. But tell me, thou witty man, hast thou a mind to sell thy clothes and leathern apron? I will give thee these gay clothes of blue and ten shillings to boot."

"Nay, thou dost jest," said the cobbler, "for my clothes are coarse and patched, and thine are of fine stuff and very pretty."

"Never a jest do I speak," quoth Robin. "I tell thee I like thy clothes well." At these words he began slipping off his doublet, and the cobbler, seeing him so in earnest, began pulling off his clothes also, for Robin Hood's garb tickled his eye. So each put on the other fellow's clothes, and Robin gave the cobbler ten bright new shillings.

Then of a sudden six horsemen burst upon them, and seized roughly upon the honest craftsman. "Ha!" roared the leader. "Have we then caught thee at last, thou blue-clad knave? Now, blessed be the name of Saint Hubert, for the good Bishop of Hereford hath promised fourscore pounds to the band that shall bring thee to him. Oho! Thou wouldst look so innocent, forsooth! We know thee, thou old fox. But off thou goest with us to have thy brush clipped forthwith." At this the poor cobbler's mouth gaped as though he had swallowed all his words.

Robin also gaped, just as the cobbler would have done in his place. "Alackadaisy, me," quoth he. "What meaneth all this stir i' th' pot, dear gentlemen? Surely this is an honest fellow."

" 'Honest fellow,' say'st thou, clown?" quoth one of the men. "Why, this is that same rogue that men call Robin Hood."

At this speech there was such a threshing of thoughts going on within the cobbler's poor head that his wits were befogged with the dust thereof. Moreover, as he saw Robin looking so like what he knew himself to be, he began to think that mayhap he was the great outlaw in real sooth. Said he in a slow, wondering voice, "Am I in truth that fellow? Now I had thought—but nay, Quince, thou art mistook—yet—am I? Nay, I must indeed be Robin Hood!"

"Alas!" quoth Robin Hood. "Look ye there, now! See how your ill-treatment hath curdled his poor wits!"

Then they tied the cobbler's hands behind him and led him off with a rope, as a farmer leads off a calf from the fair. When they were gone Robin laughed till the tears rolled down his cheeks; for he knew that no harm would befall the honest fellow, and he pictured to himself the Bishop's face when good Quince was brought before him as Robin Hood.

But Robin's journey had been hard and long, and in a se'ennight he had traveled sevenscore and more of miles. He had not gone far ere he felt his strength giving way. So, coming to an inn, he entered and bade the landlord show him to a room, although the sun was only then just sinking in the western sky. There were but two bedrooms besides his own in the place, and to the meanest one the landlord showed Robin Hood, but little Robin cared, for he could have slept that night upon a bed of broken stones. So, stripping off his clothes, he rolled into the bed and went to sleep.

Not long after, a great cloud peeped blackly over the hills to the west. Higher and higher it rose until it piled up into the night like a mountain of darkness. All around beneath it came ever and anon a dull red flash, and presently a short grim mutter of thunder was heard. Then up rode four stout burghers. Leaving their nags to the stableman, they entered the inn, and, having eaten, they bade the landlord show them to his best rooms. Then off they went, grumbling at having to sleep two in a bed; but their troubles on this score were soon lost in the quietness of sleep.

And now a gust of wind rushed past the place, banging the doors and shutters. As though the wind had brought a guest with it, the door opened and in came a rich friar of Emmet Priory. He bade the landlord first have his mule well fed and bedded in the stable, and then to bring him the very best in the house. So presently a savory stew of tripe and onions, with sweet little fat dumplings, was set before him, and the holy friar fell to with great heartiness, so that in a short time naught was left but a little pool of gravy not large enow to keep the life in a starving mouse.

Presently the rain came rattling down, beating against the casements like a hundred little hands; bright flashes of lightning lit up every raindrop, and with them came cracks of thunder. At last the holy friar bade the landlord show him to a room. When he heard that he was to bed with a cobbler, he was ill contented; he went off, grumbling like the thunder. When he came to the room, he slipped off his clothes and huddled into the bed where Robin, grunting in his sleep, made room for him. Robin was more sound asleep, I wot, than he had been for many a day, else he would never have rested so quietly with one of the friar's sort beside him. As for the friar, had he known who Robin was, you may well believe he would almost as soon have slept with an adder.

So the night passed comfortably enough, but at the first dawn of day Robin opened his eyes. Then how he stared, for there beside him lay one all shaven and shorn. Robin arose softly, and looking about the room he espied the friar's clothes upon a bench. First he looked at the clothes, with his head on one side, and then he looked at the friar and slowly winked one eye. Quoth he, "Good Brother Whate'er-thy-name-may-be, as thou hast borrowed my bed so freely I'll e'en borrow thy clothes in return." So saying, he straightway donned the holy man's garb, but kindly left the cobbler's clothes in the place of it. Then he went forth into the freshness of the morning, and the stableman asked Robin whether he wanted his mule brought from the stable.

"Yea, my son," quoth Robin—albeit he knew naught of the mule, "and bring it forth quickly, for I am late and must be jogging." So presently the stableman brought forth the mule, and Robin mounted it and went on his way rejoicing.

As for the holy friar, when he arose he raged and swore like any layman, for his rich, soft robes were gone, likewise his purse with ten golden pounds in it, and naught was left but patched clothes and a leathern apron. But as he was forced to be at Emmet

Priory that very morning, he was fain either to don the cobbler's clothes or travel the road in nakedness. So he put on the clothes and set forth afoot; but his ills had not yet done with him, for he had not gone far ere he fell into the hands of the King's men, who marched him off, willy-nilly, to Tutbury Town. In vain he swore he was a holy man, and showed his shaven crown; off he must go, for nothing would do but that he was Robin Hood.

Meanwhile Robin rode along contentedly. Now and then he passed bands of the King's men, but none of those bands stopped him, and so, at last, he reached the sweet, leafy woodlands.

Robin Hood and Guy of Gisbourne

A LONG TIME HAD PASSED since the great shooting match, and great changes had fallen in this time; for King Henry had died and King Richard had come to the crown that fitted him so well. But in Sherwood's shades Robin Hood and his men dwelt as merrily as they had ever done; for the outside world troubled them but little.

The dawning of one summer's day was fresh and bright, and the birds sang in such a tumult of sound that it awakened Robin Hood. So he rose and walked down a forest path till he came of a sudden to where a man was seated upon the mossy roots of a great oak. Robin saw that the stranger had not caught sight of him, so he stopped and looked at the other a long time. And the stranger, I wot, was well worth looking at, for from his head to his feet he was clad in a horse's hide, dressed with the hair upon it. Even the cowl that hid his face was made of the horse's skin, the ears whereof stuck up like those of a rabbit. By his side was a heavy broadsword and a double-edged dagger. A quiver of arrows hung across his shoulders, and his yew bow leaned against the tree.

"Halloa, friend," cried Robin at last, "who art thou? I make my vow I ha' never seen such a sight in all my life before."

The other answered not a word, but he pushed the cowl back from his head and showed a knit brow, a hooked nose and fierce, restless black eyes, which made Robin think of a hawk. But besides this there was something about the lines on the stranger's face, and his thin cruel mouth, that made one's flesh creep.

"What is thy name, rascal?" said he at last in a loud voice.

"As for my name," quoth Robin, "it may be this or it may be that; but methinks it is more meet for thee to tell me thine, seeing that thou art the greater stranger in these parts. Prithee, tell me, sweet chuck, why wearest thou that dainty garb?"

At these words the other broke into a short, harsh roar of laughter. "I wear this garb, thou fool, to keep my body warm," quoth he. "Likewise it is near as good as a coat of steel. As for my name, it is Guy of Gisbourne. I come from Herefordshire, upon the lands of the Bishop of that ilk. I am an outlaw, and get my living in a manner it boots not now to tell of. Not long since the Bishop sent for me, and said that if I would do a certain thing for the Sheriff of Nottingham, he would get me a free pardon, and tenscore pounds to boot. And what thinkest thou my sweet Sheriff wanted? Why, to come here to hunt up one Robin Hood and take him alive or dead. It seemeth they have no one here to face that bold fellow, and so sent all the way to Herefordshire, and to me, for thou knowest the old saying, 'Set a thief to catch a thief.' As for the slaying of this fellow, it galleth me not a whit, for I would shed the blood of my own brother for the half of two hundred pounds."

To all this Robin listened, and his gorge rose. Well he knew of this Guy of Gisbourne, and of all the bloody deeds that he had done in Herefordshire. Yet he held his peace, for he had an end to serve. "Truly," quoth he, "I have heard of thy gentle doings. Methinks there is no one in all the world that Robin Hood would rather meet than thee."

At this Guy of Gisbourne gave another harsh laugh. "Why," quoth he, "it is a merry thing to think of one stout outlaw meeting another. Only in this case it will be an ill happening for Robin Hood, for the day he meets Guy of Gisbourne he shall die."

"But, thou merry spirit," quoth Robin, "dost thou not think that mayhap this same Robin Hood may be the better man? Many think that he is one of the stoutest hereabout."

"He may be the stoutest hereabout," quoth Guy of Gisbourne,

"yet this sty of yours is not the wide world. I lay my life upon it I am the better man. Why, I hear that he hath never let blood, saving when he first came to the forest. Some call him a great archer; marry, I would not be afraid to stand against him with a bow."

"Truly, some do call him a great archer," said Robin, "but we of Nottinghamshire are famous hands with the longbow. Even I, though but a simple hand, would not fear to try a bout with thee."

"Now," quoth Guy of Gisbourne, "thou art a bold fellow. I like thy spirit in so speaking up to me, for few men have dared to do so. Put up a garland, lad, and I will try a bout with thee."

"Tut, tut," quoth Robin, "only babes shoot at garlands here-about. I will put up a good Nottingham mark for thee." So saying, he cut a hazel wand about twice the thickness of a man's thumb. From this he peeled the bark, and stuck it up in the ground fourscore paces from where the other sat. "There," quoth he. "Now let me see thee split that wand."

Then Guy of Gisbourne arose. "Now out upon it!" cried he. "The devil himself could not hit such a mark as that."

"That we shall never know till thou hast shot," quoth Robin.

At these words Guy of Gisbourne looked upon Robin with knit brows, but, as the yeoman looked innocent of any ill meaning, he bottled his words and strung his bow in silence. Twice he shot, but neither time did he hit the wand.

"Good fellow," quoth Robin, "if thou art no better with the broadsword than with the bow, thou wilt never overcome Robin Hood."

Then twice shot Robin Hood, the first time hitting within an inch of the wand, and the second time splitting it fairly in the middle. "There, thou bloody villain!" cried he, flinging his bow upon the ground. "Let that show thee how little thou knowest of manly sports. And now look thy last upon the daylight, for the good earth hath been befouled long enough by thee! This day, Our Lady willing, thou diest—I am Robin Hood." So saying, he flashed forth his bright sword in the sunlight.

"Art thou indeed?" cried Guy of Gisbourne in a wild rage. "Now I am glad to meet thee, thou poor wretch! Shrive thyself, for

thou wilt have no time for shriving when I am done with thee."
So saying, he also drew his sword.

And now came the fiercest fight that ever Sherwood saw; for
each man knew that either he or the other must die. Up and down
they fought, till at last Guy of Gisbourne made a thrust at Robin
Hood, from which Robin leaped back lightly. But in so leaping he
caught his heel in a root and fell heavily upon his back. "Now,
Holy Mary aid me!" muttered he, as the other leaped at him.
Fiercely Guy of Gisbourne stabbed with his great sword; but Robin
caught the blade in his naked hand, and, though it cut his palm, he
turned the point so that it plunged deep into the ground beside
him. Then he leaped to his feet, with his good sword in his hand,
and struck Guy of Gisbourne a backhanded blow beneath the
sword arm. Down fell the sword from Guy of Gisbourne's grasp
and back he staggered at the stroke, and, ere he could regain himself, Robin's sword passed through his body. Around he spun, and,
flinging his hands aloft with a shrill, wild cry, fell upon his face.

Then Robin wiped his sword and thrust it back into the scabbard, and he stood over Guy of Gisbourne with folded arms, talking to himself: This is the first man I have slain since I shot the
King's forester in the hot days of my youth. I think bitterly, even
yet, of that first life I took, but of this I am as glad as though I had
slain a wild boar. Since the Sheriff hath sent such a one as this
against me, I will put on the fellow's garb and go to find his worship, and perchance pay him the debt I owe upon this score.

So saying, Robin put on the hairy garments, all bloody as they
were. Then, strapping the other's sword and dagger around his
body and carrying his own in his hand, together with the two yew
bows, he drew the cowl of horse's hide over his face and set forth
toward Nottingham Town. As he strode along the country roads,
men, women and children hid away from him, for the terror of
Guy of Gisbourne's doings had spread far and near.

Now WHILE THESE THINGS were happening, Little John also had
been walking through the forest paths, until he had come to the
highroad where a little thatched cottage stood back of a cluster

of twisted crab-apple trees. Here he thought that he heard the sound of someone in sorrow; so he pushed open the wicket and entered the cottage. There he saw a gray-haired dame rocking herself to and fro and weeping bitterly.

Now Little John had a tender heart for the sorrows of other folk, so, patting the old woman kindly upon the shoulder, he bade her tell him her troubles. So the good dame told him all that bore upon her mind. That that morning she had three as fair, tall sons beside her as one could find in all Nottinghamshire, but that they were now taken from her, and were like to be hanged; that, want having come upon them, her eldest boy, the night before, had slain a hind in the forest; that the King's rangers had followed the blood upon the grass until they had come to her cottage, and had there found the deer's meat in the cupboard; that, as neither of the younger sons would betray their brother, the foresters had taken all three away, in spite of the eldest's saying that he alone had slain the deer; that, as they went, she had heard the rangers saying that the Sheriff had sworn that he would put a check upon the slaughter of deer that had been going on of late by hanging the first rogue caught thereat upon the nearest tree, and that they would take the three youths to the King's Head Inn, near Nottingham Town, where the Sheriff was abiding that day.

"Alas," quoth Little John, "this is indeed an ill case. No time may be lost if we would save their lives. Tell me, hast thou any clothes hereabout that I may put on in place of these? Marry, if our Sheriff catcheth me without disguise, I am like to be run up more quickly than thy sons."

Then the woman brought some of the clothes of her husband, who had died only two years before; and Little John, doffing his garb of Lincoln green, put them on in its stead. Then, making a wig and false beard of uncarded wool, he covered his own brown hair and beard, and, putting on a tall hat that had belonged to the old peasant, he took his staff in one hand and his bow in the other, and set forth.

At the cozy inn bearing the Sign of the King's Head there was a great bustle and stir, for the Sheriff and his men had come there to await Guy of Gisbourne's return from the forest. The Sheriff sat within, feasting merrily, and the Sheriff's men sat upon the bench before the door, quaffing ale. All around stood the horses of the band, with a great noise of stamping feet and a great switching of tails. To this inn came the King's rangers, driving the widow's sons before them. The hands of the three youths were tied tightly behind their backs, and a cord from neck to neck fastened them all together. So they were marched to where the Sheriff sat at meat, and stood trembling before him.

"So," quoth he, in an angry voice, "ye have been poaching upon the King's deer? Now I will hang up all three of you as a farmer would hang up three crows to scare others of the kind."

Then the Sheriff bade the rangers to take the poor youths away till he had done his eating. So they were marched outside, where they stood with bowed heads and despairing hearts, till after a while the Sheriff came forth. Then he called his men about him, and quoth he, "We will take these three villains over yonder to that belt of woodlands, for I would fain hang them upon the very trees of Sherwood itself, to show those vile outlaws therein what they may expect of me if I ever have the good luck to lay hands upon them." So saying, he mounted his horse, as did his men-at-arms, and all together they set forth for the woodlands, the poor youths walking in their midst. So they came at last to the spot, and here nooses were fastened around the necks of the three, and the ends of the cords flung over the branch of a great oak tree.

While all this had been going forward, an old man had drawn near and stood leaning on his staff, looking on. His hair and beard were all curly and white, and across his back was a bow of yew that looked much too strong for him to draw. The Sheriff's eyes fell upon this strange old man, and he beckoned to him. So Little John, for it was none other, came forward, and the Sheriff, thinking there was something strangely familiar in the face, said, "Methinks I have seen thee before. What may thy name be, father?"

"Please your worship," said Little John, in a cracked voice like that of an old man, "my name is Giles Hobble."

"Giles Hobble, Giles Hobble," muttered the Sheriff. "I remember not thy name, but it matters not. Hast thou a mind to earn sixpence this bright morn?"

"Aye, marry," quoth Little John, "for money is not so plenty with me that I should cast sixpence away an I could earn it by an honest turn. What is it your worship would have me do?"

"Why, this," said the Sheriff. "Here are three men that need hanging as badly as any e'er I saw. If thou wilt string them up I will pay thee twopence apiece for them. I like not that my men-at-arms should turn hangmen. Wilt thou try thy hand?"

"Insooth," said Little John, "I ha' never done such a thing before; but an a sixpence is to be earned I might as well ha' it as anybody. But, your worship, are these fellows shrived?"

"Nay," said the Sheriff, laughing, "never a whit; but thou may'st turn thy hand to that also if thou art so minded."

So Little John came to where the youths stood trembling, and, putting his face to the first fellow's cheek as though he were listening to him, he whispered softly, "Stand still, brother, when thou feelest thy bonds cut, but when thou see'st me throw aside my woolen wig and beard, cast the noose from thy neck and run for the woodlands." Then he slyly cut the cord that bound the youth's hands; who, upon his part, stood still as though he were yet bound. Then he spoke to the second fellow in the same way, and also cut his bonds. This he did to the third likewise.

Then Little John turned to the Sheriff. "Please your worship," said he, "will you give me leave to string my bow? For I would fain help these fellows along the way, when they are swinging, with an arrow beneath the ribs."

"With all my heart," said the Sheriff, "only make haste."

Little John put the tip of his bow to his instep, and strung the weapon so deftly that all wondered to see an old man so strong. Next he drew an arrow from his quiver and fitted it to the string; then he cast away the wool from his head and face, shouting in a mighty voice, "Run!" Quick as a flash the three youths flung the nooses from their necks and sped across the open to the woodlands. Little John also flew toward the covert, while the Sheriff and his men gazed after him all bewildered with the sudden doing. But ere the yeoman had gone far the Sheriff roused himself. "After him!" he roared; for he knew now who it was.

When Little John heard the Sheriff's words, he stopped and turned suddenly, holding his bow as though he were about to shoot. "Stand back!" cried he fiercely. "The first man that cometh a foot forward dieth!"

At these words the Sheriff's men stood as still as stocks. In vain the Sheriff urged them forward; they would not budge an inch, but watched Little John as he moved slowly toward the forest, keeping his gaze fixed upon them. But when the Sheriff saw his enemy thus slipping betwixt his fingers he grew mad with rage. So, plunging his spurs into his horse's sides, he gave a great shout, rose in his stirrups and came down upon Little John like the wind. Then Little John raised his bow and drew the gray goose feather to his cheek. But alas! Ere he could loose the shaft, the good bow that had served him so long split in his hands, and the arrow fell harmless at his feet. Seeing this, the Sheriff, leaning forward, struck Little John a mighty blow. Little John ducked and the Sheriff's sword turned in his hand, but the flat of the blade struck the other upon the head and smote him down, senseless.

"Now, I am right glad," said the Sheriff, when the men came up and found that Little John was not dead, "that I have not slain this man in my haste! I would rather lose five hundred pounds than have him die thus instead of hanging." Presently Little John opened his eyes and looked around him, all dazed and bewildered. Then they tied his hands behind him, and set him upon the back of one of the horses, with his face to its tail and his feet strapped beneath its belly. And so they took him back toward the inn.

Now the Sheriff's heart rejoiced. Quoth he to himself, This time tomorrow the rogue shall hang upon the gallows tree in front of the great gate of Nottingham Town. But then the Sheriff shook his head and muttered to himself, Should his master escape Guy of Gisbourne, there is no knowing what he may do. Belike I had better not wait until tomorrow. So he said to his men, "This rogue shall be hanged forthwith, and that from the very tree whence he saved those three young villains."

So, one leading the horse whereon Little John sat and the others riding around him, they went back to that tree from the branches of which they had thought to hang the poachers. Here one of the men spoke to the Sheriff of a sudden. "Your worship," cried he, "is not yon fellow coming toward us that same Guy of Gisbourne whom thou didst send to seek Robin Hood?"

The Sheriff shaded his eyes and looked. "Why, certes," quoth he, "yon fellow is the same. Now, heaven send that he hath slain the master thief, as we will presently slay the man!"

When Little John heard this speech he looked up, and straightway his heart crumbled within him, for not only were the man's garments all covered with blood, but he wore Robin Hood's bugle horn and carried his bow and broadsword.

"How now!" cried the Sheriff, when Robin Hood, in Guy of Gisbourne's clothes, had come nigh to them. "What luck hath befallen thee? Why, man, thy clothes are all over blood!"

"An thou likest not my clothes," said Robin in a harsh voice like that of Guy of Gisbourne, "thou may'st shut thine eyes. Marry, the blood upon me is that of the vilest outlaw that ever trod the woodlands, and one whom I have slain this day."

Then out spoke Little John, for the first time since he had fallen into the Sheriff's hands. "Oh thou bloody wretch! Is it by such a hand as thine that the gentlest heart that ever beat is stilled? Truly, thou art a fit tool for this coward Sheriff. Now care I not how I die, for life is naught to me!"

But the Sheriff laughed for joy. "This is a good day!" cried he. "The great outlaw dead and his right-hand man in my hands! Ask what thou wilt, Guy of Gisbourne, and it is thine!"

"Then this I ask," said Robin. "As I have slain the master I would now kill the man. Give this fellow's life into my hands."

"Now thou art a fool!" cried the Sheriff. "Thou might'st have had money enough for a knight's ransom if thou hadst asked for it. I like ill to let this fellow pass from my hands, but as I have promised, thou shalt have him."

"I thank thee right heartily," cried Robin. "Take the rogue down from the horse, men, and lean him against yonder tree."

While the Sheriff's men were doing this Robin strung both his bow and that of Guy of Gisbourne, albeit none of them took notice of his doing so. Then, when Little John stood against the tree, Robin drew Guy of Gisbourne's dagger. "Fall back! Fall back!" cried he. "Would ye crowd so on my pleasure, ye unmannerly knaves? Back, I say! Farther yet!"

"Come!" cried Little John. "Here is my breast. It is meet that the hand that slew my dear master should butcher me also!"

"Peace, Little John!" said Robin in a low voice. "Couldst thou not tell me beneath this beast's hide? Just in front of thee lie my bow and arrows, likewise my broadsword. Take them when I cut thy bonds. Now!" So saying, he cut the bonds, and Little John, quick as a wink, caught up the bow and arrows and the broadsword. At the same time Robin Hood threw back the cowl from his face and bent Guy of Gisbourne's bow, with a keen, barbed arrow fitted to the string. "Stand back!" cried he sternly. "The first man that toucheth finger to bowstring dieth! I have slain thy man, Sheriff; take heed that it is not thy turn next." Then, seeing that Little John had armed himself, he clapped his horn to his lips and blew three blasts both loud and shrill.

Now when the Sheriff saw whose face it was beneath Guy of Gisbourne's hood, and when he heard those bugle notes ring in his ear, he felt as if his hour had come. "Robin Hood!" roared he, and without another word he wheeled his horse and went off in a cloud of dust. The Sheriff's men, seeing their master thus fleeing, clapped spurs to their horses and dashed away after him. But though the Sheriff went fast, he could not outstrip a cloth-yard arrow. Little John twanged his bowstring with a shout, and when the Sheriff dashed in through the gates of Nottingham Town it was with a gray goose shaft sticking out behind him, like a molting sparrow with one feather in its tail. For a month afterward the poor Sheriff could sit upon naught but the softest cushions.

Thus it was that when Will Stutely and a dozen yeomen burst from out the covert, they saw the Sheriff and his men scurrying away in the distance. Then they all went back into the forest, where they found the widow's three sons, who ran to Little John and kissed his hands. But it would not do for them to roam the forest at large anymore; so they promised that, after they had told their mother of their escape, they would return to the greenwood tree and thenceforth become men of the band.

King Richard Comes to Sherwood Forest

NOT MORE THAN TWO MONTHS after these adventures all Nottinghamshire was in a mighty stir and tumult, for King Richard of the Lion's Heart was making a royal progress through merry England, and his Majesty was to stop in Nottingham Town, as the guest of the Sheriff. A rapping of hammers and a babble of voices sounded through the place, for the folk were building great arches across the streets, and were draping these arches with banners and streamers of many colors. A grand banquet was to be given in the Guild Hall to the King and his nobles.

At last the day came that should bring the King into the town, and bright shone the sun down into the stony streets. On either side of the way great crowds of folk stood packed as close as dried herring in a box, so that the Sheriff's men could hardly press them back to leave space for the King's riding.

And now a gallant array of men came into sight, and the cheering of the people ran down the crowd as the fire runs in dry grass. Eight and twenty heralds in velvet and cloth of gold came riding forward, each herald bearing in his hand a long silver trumpet, which he blew musically. From each trumpet hung a heavy banner with the royal arms of England emblazoned thereon. After these came riding fivescore noble knights, two by two, all fully armed, saving that their heads were uncovered. In their hands they bore tall lances, from the tops of which fluttered pennons of many colors and devices. By the side of each knight walked a page, bearing in his hands his master's helmet, from which waved long, floating plumes of feathers. Behind the knights came the barons and the nobles of the mid-country; behind these again came men-at-arms, with spears and halberds in their hands, and, in the midst of these, two riders side by side. One was the Sheriff of Nottingham in his robes of office. The other, who was a head taller than the Sheriff, was clad in a rich but simple garb, with a heavy chain about his neck. His hair and beard were like threads of gold, and his eyes were as blue as the summer sky. As he rode along he bowed to the right and the left, and a mighty roar of voices followed him as he passed; for this was King Richard.

Then, above the tumult, a great voice was heard. "Heaven, its saints bless thee, our gracious King Richard!" Then the King, looking toward the spot whence the sound came, saw a tall, burly priest standing in front of all the crowd with his legs wide apart.

"By my soul, Sheriff," said King Richard, laughing, "ye have here the tallest priests that e'er I saw in all my life."

At this all the blood left the Sheriff's cheeks, and he caught at the pommel of his saddle to keep himself from falling; for he knew the tall priest to be Friar Tuck; and behind Friar Tuck he saw the faces of Robin Hood and others of the band.

"How now," said the King hastily, "art thou ill, Sheriff, that thou growest so white?"

"Nay, your Majesty," said the Sheriff, "it was but a sudden pain that will soon pass by." For he was ashamed that the King should know that Robin Hood feared him so little that he thus dared to come within the very gates of Nottingham Town.

Thus rode the King into Nottingham; and none rejoiced more than Robin and his men to see him come so royally unto his own.

EVENTIDE HAD COME; the great feast in the Guild Hall at Nottingham Town was done, and the wine passed freely. At the head of the table, upon a throne all hung with cloth of gold, sat King Richard with the Sheriff beside him. Quoth the King, laughing as he spoke, "I have heard much spoken concerning the doings of certain outlaws hereabout, one Robin Hood and his band. Canst thou not tell me somewhat of them, Sir Sheriff?"

At these words the Sheriff looked down gloomily. "I can tell your Majesty but little concerning those fellows," quoth he, "saving that they are the boldest lawbreakers in all the land."

Then up spoke young Sir Henry of the Lea, a favorite with the King, under whom he had fought in Palestine. "May it please your Majesty," said he, "I have heard ofttimes from my father of this Robin Hood." Then he told how Robin had aided Sir Richard with money borrowed from the Bishop of Hereford. The King roared with laughter, while the Bishop, who was present, waxed cherry-red in the face. Then others, seeing how the King enjoyed this tale, told other tales of Robin and his men.

"By the hilt of my sword," said King Richard, "this is as merry a knave as ever I heard tell of. Marry, I must do what thou couldst not do, Sheriff, to wit, clear the forest of his band."

That night the King sat in the place that was set apart for his lodging while in Nottingham Town. With him were young Sir Henry of the Lea and two other knights and three barons of Nottinghamshire; but the King's mind still dwelt upon Robin Hood. "Now," quoth he, "I would give a hundred pounds to meet this fellow, and to see somewhat of his doings."

Then up spoke Sir Hubert of Bingham, laughing. "Such a desire is not so hard to satisfy, if your Majesty is willing to lose one hundred pounds. Let us put on the robes of the Order of Black Friars, and let your Majesty hang a purse of one hundred pounds beneath your gown; then let us ride from here to Mansfield Town tomorrow, and, without I am much mistaken, we will both meet with Robin Hood and dine with him."

"I like thy plan, Sir Hubert," quoth the King merrily, "and tomorrow we will try it and see whether there be virtue in it."

So it happened that when early the next morning the Sheriff came to his liege lord to pay his duty to him, the King told him what merry adventure they were set upon undertaking. "Alas!" said the Sheriff. "My gracious lord, you know not what you do! This villain hath no reverence either for king or king's laws."

"But did I not hear aright that this Robin Hood hath shed no blood since he was outlawed, saving only that of that vile Guy of Gisbourne, for whose death all honest men should thank him?"

"Yea, your Majesty," said the Sheriff. "Nevertheless—"

"Then," quoth the King, breaking in on the Sheriff's speech, "what have I to fear in meeting him, having done him no harm? But mayhap thou wilt go with us, Sir Sheriff."

"Nay," quoth the Sheriff hastily. "Heaven forbid!"

But now seven habits such as Black Friars wear were brought, and the King and those about him having clad themselves therein, and his Majesty having hung a purse with a hundred golden pounds in it beneath his robes, they all mounted on mules and so set forth upon their way. Onward they traveled till they came within the heavy shade of the forest itself.

"By the holy Saint Martin," quoth the King. "Here have we come away and brought never a drop of anything to drink. Now I would give half a hundred pounds for somewhat to quench my thirst."

No sooner had the King so spoken, than out from the covert at the roadside stepped a tall fellow with yellow beard and hair and a pair of merry blue eyes. "Truly, holy brother," said he, laying his hand upon the King's bridle rein, "it were unchristian not to give fitting answer to so fair a bargain. We keep an inn hereabout, and for fifty pounds we will not only give thee a good draught of wine, but will give thee as noble a feast as ever did tickle thy gullet." So saying, he put his fingers to his lips and blew a shrill whistle. Then straightway threescore yeomen in Lincoln green burst out of the covert.

"How now," quoth the King, "who art thou, thou naughty rogue? Hast thou no regard for such holy men as we are?"

"Not a whit," quoth the merry fellow, "for insooth, all the holiness belonging to rich friars, such as ye are, one could drop into a thimble and the goodwife would never feel it with the tip of her finger. As for my name, it is Robin Hood."

"Now out upon thee!" quoth King Richard. "Thou art a bold and lawless fellow, as I have often heard tell. Now, prithee, let me, and these brethren of mine, travel forward in peace."

"It may not be," said Robin, "for it would look but ill of us to let such holy men travel onward with empty stomachs. But I doubt not that thou hast a fat purse to pay thy score at our inn, since thou offerest freely so much for a poor draught of wine. Show me thy purse, reverend brother, or I may perchance have to strip thy robes from thee to search for it myself."

"Nay, use no force," said the King sternly. "Here is my purse, but lay not thy lawless hands upon our person."

"Hut, tut," quoth Robin, "what proud words are these? Art thou the King of England, to talk so? Here, Will, take this purse and see what there is within."

Will Scarlet took the purse and counted out the money. Then Robin bade him keep fifty pounds, and put fifty back into the purse. This he handed to the King. "Here, brother," quoth he, "take this and thank Saint Martin, on whom thou didst call, that thou hast fallen into the hands of such gentle rogues. But wilt thou not put back thy cowl? For I would fain see thy face."

"Nay," said the King, drawing back, "for we seven have vowed that we will not show our faces for four and twenty hours."

"Then keep them covered in peace," said Robin, "and far be it from me to make you break your vows."

So he bade seven of his men each take a mule by the bridle; then they journeyed on until they came to the greenwood tree, where Friar Tuck and twoscore or more stout yeomen abided them.

"By my soul," quoth King Richard, looking about him, "thou hast in truth a fine lot of young men about thee, Robin. Methinks King Richard himself would be glad of such a bodyguard."

"These are not all of my fellows," said Robin proudly, "for threescore more of them are away on business. But, as for King Richard, I tell thee, brother, there is not a man of us all but would pour out our blood like water for him. Ye churchmen cannot rightly understand our King; but we yeomen love him for the sake of his brave doings."

But now Friar Tuck came bustling up. "Gi' ye good den, brothers," said he. "I am right glad to welcome some of my cloth in this naughty place. Methinks these rogues of outlaws would stand but an ill chance were it not for the prayers of holy Tuck." Here he winked slyly and stuck his tongue into his cheek.

"Who art thou, mad priest?" said the King in a serious voice, albeit he smiled beneath his cowl.

At this Friar Tuck gazed around. "Look you now," quoth he, "never let me hear you say again that I am no patient man. Here is a knave of a friar calleth me a mad priest, and yet I smite him not. My name is Friar Tuck, fellow—the holy Friar Tuck."

"There, Tuck," said Robin, "cease thy talk and bring some wine. These reverend men are athirst, and sin' they have paid so richly for their score they must e'en have the best."

Friar Tuck bridled at being so checked; nevertheless he went. So presently a great crock was brought, and wine was poured out for all. Then Robin held his cup aloft. "Here is to good King Richard," cried he, "and may all enemies to him be confounded!"

Then all drank to the King, even the King himself. "Methinks," said he, "thou hast drunk to thine own confusion."

"Never a whit," quoth Robin, "for I tell thee that we are more loyal than those of thine order. We would give up our lives for the King while ye lie snug in your abbeys, let reign who will."

At this the King laughed. Quoth he, "Perhaps King Richard's welfare is more to me than thou wottest of. But enough of that matter. I have oft heard that ye are wondrous archers. Wilt thou not show us somewhat of your skill?"

"With all my heart," said Robin. "Ho, lads! Set up a garland at the end of the glade, and each of you shoot three arrows thereat. If any fellow misseth, he shall have a buffet of Will Scarlet's fist."

"Why, master," quoth Friar Tuck, "thou dost bestow buffets from thy strapping nephew as though they were love taps from some bouncing lass."

First David of Doncaster shot, and lodged all of his arrows within the garland. Next Midge, the Miller's son, shot, and he also lodged his arrows in the garland. Then followed Wat, the Tinker, but one of his shafts missed by the breadth of two fingers.

"Come hither, fellow," said Will Scarlet, in his gentle voice. Then Wat stood in front of Will Scarlet, screwing up his face, and as though he already felt his ears ringing with the buffet. Will Scarlet rolled up his sleeve, and, standing on tiptoe, struck with might and main. *Whoof!* came his palm against the tinker's head, and down went stout Wat to the grass, heels over head.

Then, as the tinker sat up upon the grass, blinking at the bright stars that danced before his eyes, the yeomen roared with mirth. As for King Richard, he laughed till the tears ran down his cheeks. Thus the band shot, each in turn, some getting off scot-free, and some winning a buffet that always sent them to the grass. And now, last of all, Robin took his place. The first shaft he shot split a piece from the stake on which the garland was hung; the second lodged within an inch of the other. And now, for the third time Robin shot; but alas for him! The arrow was ill feathered, and, wavering to one side, it smote an inch outside the garland.

At this the yeomen shouted with laughter, for never before had they seen their master miss his mark; but Robin flung his bow upon the ground. "Now, out upon it!" cried he. "That shaft had an ill feather. Give me a clean arrow, and I will engage to split the wand with it."

"Nay, good Uncle," said Will Scarlet, "I swear the arrow was as good as any that hath been loosed this day. Come hither; I owe thee somewhat, and would fain pay it."

"Go, good master," roared Friar Tuck, "and my blessing go with thee. Thou hast bestowed Will Scarlet's love taps with great freedom. It were pity an thou gottest not thine own share."

"It may not be," said Robin. "I am king here, and no subject may raise hand against the king. But even great King Richard may yield to the holy Pope without shame; therefore I will yield myself to this holy friar." Thus saying, he turned to the King. "I prithee, brother, wilt thou take my punishing into thy hands?"

"With all my heart," quoth King Richard, rising. "I owe thee somewhat for having lifted a heavy weight from my purse."

"An thou makest me tumble," quoth Robin, "I will freely give thee back thy fifty pounds."

"So be it," said the King. Thereupon he rolled up his sleeve and showed an arm that made the yeomen stare. But Robin, with his feet wide apart, stood firmly planted, waiting the other, smiling. Then the King swung back his arm, and delivered a buffet that fell like a thunderbolt, and down went Robin headlong upon the grass. Then how the yeomen laughed, for never had they seen such a buffet given. As for Robin, he presently sat up and looked all around him, as though he had dropped from a cloud and had lit in a place he had never seen before. After a while, he put his fingertips softly to his ear and felt all around it tenderly. "Will Scarlet," said he, "count this fellow out his fifty pounds; I want nothing more either of his money or of him. I would that I had taken my dues from thee, for I verily believe he hath deafened mine ear from ever hearing again."

Then Will Scarlet counted out the fifty pounds, and the King dropped it into his purse again. "I give thee thanks, fellow," said he, "and if ever thou shouldst wish for another box of the ear, come to me and I will fit thee with it for naught."

Even as the King ended, there came suddenly the sound of many voices, and out from the covert burst Little John and threescore men, with Sir Richard of the Lea in the midst. "Make haste, dear friend," Sir Richard shouted to Robin, "gather thy band together and come with me! A rumor has reached me that King Richard left Nottingham Town this very morning, and cometh to seek thee in the woodlands. Therefore hasten to Castle Lea, for there thou may'st lie hidden till thy present danger passeth. Who are these strangers that thou hast with thee?"

"Why," quoth Robin, rising from the grass, "these are certain gentle guests that I met with on the highroad. I know not their names."

Sir Richard looked keenly at the tall friar, who, drawing himself up to his full height, looked fixedly back at the knight. Then Sir Richard's cheeks grew pale, for he knew who it was that he looked upon. Quickly he leaped from off his horse and flung himself upon his knees before the other. At this, the King threw back his cowl, and all the yeomen knew him also, for there was not one of them but had seen him riding in Nottingham with the Sheriff. Down they fell upon their knees, nor could they say a word. Then the King looked all around right grimly, and, last of all, his glance rested again upon Sir Richard.

"How is this, Sir Richard?" said he. "How darest thou offer thy knightly castle for a refuge to these outlaws?"

Then Sir Richard raised his eyes to the King's face. "Far be it from me," said he, "to do aught that could bring your Majesty's anger upon me. Yet, sooner would I face your Majesty's wrath than suffer aught of harm to fall upon Robin Hood and his band; for to them I owe life, honor, everything."

Ere the knight had done speaking, one of the mock friars came forward and knelt beside Sir Richard, and throwing back his cowl showed the face of young Sir Henry of the Lea. Then Sir Henry grasped his father's hand and said, "Here kneels one, King Richard, who hath stepped between thee and death in Palestine; yet here I say also, that I would freely give shelter to this noble outlaw, even though it brought thy wrath upon me, for my father's honor and welfare are as dear to me as mine own."

King Richard looked from one to the other of the kneeling knights, and the frown faded from his brow. "Sir Richard," quoth he, "thou art a bold-spoken knight, and thy son taketh after his sire in boldness of speech and of deed, for, as he sayeth, he stepped one time betwixt me and death; wherefore I would pardon thee for his sake even if thou hadst done more than thou hast. Rise all of you, for ye shall suffer no harm through me this day; it were pity that a merry time should end in a manner as to mar its joyousness."

Then the King beckoned to Robin Hood and said, with something of sternness in his voice, "Take not thy sins lightly, good Robin; but now come, look up. I hereby give thee and all thy band free pardon. I will take thee at thy word, when thou didst say thou wouldst give thy service to me, and thou shalt go back to London with me. We will take that bold knave Little John also, and thy cousin, Will Scarlet, and thy minstrel, Allan a Dale. As for the rest of thy band, we will have them duly recorded as royal rangers; for methinks it were wiser to have them changed to law-abiding caretakers of our deer in Sherwood than to leave them to run at large as outlawed slayers thereof. But now get a feast ready; I would see how ye live in the woodlands."

So straightway great fires were kindled and burned brightly, at which savory things roasted sweetly. While this was going forward, Allan a Dale sang and played upon his harp for the King. Then

King Richard feasted and drank, and when he was done he swore roundly that he had never sat at such a lusty repast in all his life.

That night he lay in Sherwood Forest upon a bed of sweet green leaves, and early the next morning he set forth for Nottingham Town, Robin Hood and all of his band going with him. You may guess what a stir there was in the town when all these famous outlaws came marching into the streets. As for the Sheriff, he knew not what to say when he saw Robin Hood in such high favor with the King, and all his heart was filled with gall.

The next day Robin Hood and Little John and Will Scarlet and Allan a Dale shook hands with all the rest of the band, kissing the cheeks of each man, and swearing that they would come often to Sherwood. Then each mounted his horse and they rode away in the train of the King.

EPILOGUE

THUS END THE MERRY ADVENTURES of Robin Hood; for, in spite of his promise, it was many a year ere he saw Sherwood again.

After a year or two at court Little John came back to Nottinghamshire, where he lived in an orderly way, though within sight of Sherwood, and where he achieved fame as the champion of all England with the quarterstaff. Will Scarlet after a time came back to his own home, whence he had been driven by his unlucky killing of his father's steward. The rest of the band did their duty as royal rangers right well. But Robin (and Allan a Dale) did not come again to Sherwood so quickly, for Robin, through his great fame as an archer, speedily rose in rank to be the chief of all the yeomen, and the King, seeing how faithful he was, created him Earl of Huntingdon; so Robin followed the King to the wars, and had no chance to come back to Sherwood.

And now, dear friend, I will tell as speedily as may be of how that stout fellow died as he had lived, not at court, but with bow in hand, and his heart in the greenwood.

King Richard died upon the battlefield, in such a way as properly became a lionhearted king; so, after a time, the Earl of Huntingdon—or Robin Hood, as we still call him—finding nothing for his doing abroad, came back to England. With him came Allan a Dale and his wife, the fair Ellen, for these two had been chief of Robin's household ever since he had left Sherwood Forest.

It was in the springtime when they landed on the shores of England. The leaves were green and the small birds sang blithely, just as they used to do in Sherwood when Robin roamed the forest, so that a great longing came upon him to behold the woodlands once more. So he went to King John and besought leave to visit Nottingham. The King gave him leave, but bade him not stay longer than three days. So Robin and Allan a Dale set forth.

At Nottingham Town they took up their inn, yet they did not pay their duty to the Sheriff, for his worship's bitter grudge had not been lessened by Robin's rise in the world. The next day they set forth for the woodlands. As they rode along it seemed to Robin that he knew every stick and stone that his eyes looked upon. Yonder was a path that he had ofttimes trod of a mellow evening, with Little John beside him; here was one, now nigh choked with brambles, along which he and a little band had walked when they went forth to seek a certain curtal friar.

At last they came to the open glade, and the widespreading greenwood tree which was their home for so many years. Robin looked all about him at the well-known things, so like what they used to be and yet so different; for where once was the bustle of many busy fellows was now the quietness of solitude; and, as he looked, the woodlands, the greensward and the sky all blurred together in his sight through salt tears.

That morning he had slung his good old bugle horn over his shoulder, and now came a longing to sound his bugle once more. He raised it to his lips; he blew a blast. *Tirila, lirila*, the sweet, clear notes went winding down the forest paths, coming back again from the more distant bosky shades in faint echoes, *Tirila, lirila, tirila, lirila*, until it faded away and was lost.

Now it chanced that on that very morn Little John was walking through a spur of the forest upon a matter of business when the

faint, clear notes of a distant bugle horn came to his ear. All the
blood in Little John's body seemed to rush like a flame into his
cheeks as he bent his head and listened. Again came the bugle note,
thin and clear, and yet again it sounded. Then Little John gave a
wild cry of joy and yet of grief, and putting down his head, he
dashed into the thicket. Onward he plunged, through the under-
brush, little recking he of thorns and briers that scratched his
flesh and tore his clothing, for all he thought of was to get, by the
shortest way, to the greenwood glade whence the sound of the
bugle horn came. Out he burst from the covert, at last, a shower of
little broken twigs falling about him, and rushed forward and
flung himself at Robin's feet. Then he clasped his arms around the
master's knees, and all his body was shaken with sobs; neither
could Robin nor Allan a Dale speak, but stood looking down at
Little John, the tears rolling down their cheeks.

While they thus stood, seven royal rangers rushed into the open
glade and raised a great shout of joy at the sight of Robin; and at
their head was Will Stutely. Then, after a while, came four more,
and one was Midge, the Miller's son; for all of these had heard the
sound of Robin Hood's horn.

Robin looked around him and said, in a husky voice, "Now, I
swear that never again will I leave these dear woodlands. I have
been away from them and from you too long. Now do I lay by
the name of Robert, Earl of Huntingdon, and take upon me once
again that nobler title, Robin Hood, the Yeoman." At this all the
yeomen shouted and shook one another's hands for joy.

The news that Robin Hood had come back to dwell in Sherwood as of old spread like wildfire all over the countryside, so
that ere a se'ennight had passed nearly all of his old yeomen had
gathered about him again. But when the news of this reached King
John, he swore both loud and deep and took a solemn vow that
he would not rest until he had Robin Hood in his power, dead or
alive. Now there was a certain knight, Sir William Dale, who was
head keeper over that part of Sherwood Forest that lay nigh to
Mansfield Town; so the King bade him take an army of men, and
the Sheriff also, and go straightway to seek Robin Hood. So Sir

William and the Sheriff set forth to do the King's bidding; and for seven days they hunted Robin up and down, and yet found him not.

Now, had Robin Hood been as peaceful as of old, everything might have ended in smoke, as other such ventures had always done before; but he had fought for years under King Richard, and it galled his pride thus to flee, as a chased fox flees from the hounds; so it came about, at last, that Robin and his yeomen met Sir William and the Sheriff and their men in the forest, and a bloody fight followed. The first man slain was the Sheriff of Nottingham, for he fell from his horse with an arrow in his brain ere half a score of shafts had been sped. Many a better man than the Sheriff kissed the sod that day, but at last, Sir William Dale being wounded and most of his men slain, he withdrew, beaten, and left the forest. Scores of good fellows were left behind him, stretched out all stiff beneath the sweet green boughs.

But though Robin Hood had beaten off his enemies in fair fight, all this lay heavily upon his mind, so that he brooded over it until a fever seized upon him. For three days it held him, and though he strove to fight it off, he was forced to yield at last. On the morning of the fourth day, he bade Little John go with him to his cousin, the prioress of the nunnery near Kirklees, in Yorkshire, who was a skillful leech; he would have her open a vein in his arm and take a little blood from him, for the bettering of his health. Little John and he took their leave of the others, and Robin Hood bade Will Stutely be the captain of the band until they should come back. Thus they came by easy stages and slow journeying to Kirklees.

Now Robin had done much to aid this cousin of his; for it was through King Richard's love of him that she had been made prioress of the place. But there is naught in the world so easily forgot as gratitude; so, when the Prioress of Kirklees had heard how her cousin, the Earl of Huntingdon, had thrown away his earldom and gone back again to Sherwood, she feared lest her cousinship with him should bring the King's wrath upon her also. Thus it happened that when Robin came to her and told her how he wished her services as leech, she began plotting ill against him in her mind, thinking that by doing evil to him she might find favor with his enemies. Nevertheless, she received Robin with seeming kindness. She led him up the winding stone stair to a room which was just beneath the eaves of a high, round tower; but she would not let Little John come with him.

So the poor yeoman left his master in the hands of the women. But he did not go far away; for he laid him down in a glade near-by, where he could watch the place, like some great, faithful dog turned away from the door where his master had entered.

After the women had gotten Robin Hood to the room beneath the eaves, the Prioress sent all of the others away; then, taking a little cord, she tied it tightly about Robin's arm, as though she were about to bleed him, but the vein she opened was not one of those that lie close and blue beneath the skin; but one of those through which the bright red blood runs leaping from the heart.

Having done this vile deed, the Prioress left her cousin, locking the door behind her. All that day the blood ran from Robin's arm, nor could he check it, though he strove in every way to do so. Again and again he called for help, but no help came, for his cousin had betrayed him, and Little John was too far away to hear his voice. So he bled and bled until he felt his strength slipping away from him. Then he arose, tottering, and bearing himself up by the palms of his hands against the wall, he reached his bugle horn at last. Thrice he sounded it, but faintly, for his breath was fluttering through loss of strength; nevertheless, Little John heard it where he lay in the glade, and, with a heart all sick with dread, he came running toward the nunnery. Loudly he knocked at the the door, and shouted for them to let him in; but the door was of massive oak, strongly barred, and studded with spikes, so they felt safe, and bade Little John begone.

Then Little John looked wildly about him, and his sight fell upon a heavy stone mortar, such as three men could not lift now-adays. Little John took three steps forward, and, bending his back, heaved the stone mortar up from where it stood deeply rooted. Staggering under its weight, he came forward and hurled it against the door. In burst the door, and away fled the frightened nuns, shrieking. Then Little John strode in, and up the winding stone steps he ran to the room wherein his master was. Here he found the door locked also, but, putting his shoulder against it, he burst the locks as though they were made of brittle ice.

There he saw his own dear master leaning against the stone wall, his face all white and drawn, and his head swaying to and fro with weakness. Then, with a great cry of grief and pity, Little John caught Robin Hood in his arms. Up he lifted him as a mother lifts her child, and laid him tenderly on the bed.

And now the Prioress came in hastily, for she was frightened at what she had done, and dreaded the vengeance of Little John and the band; then she stanched the blood by cunning bandages, so that it flowed no more. And after she had done, Little John sternly bade her to begone, and she obeyed, pale and trembling.

Then Little John spoke cheering words, saying that no stout yeoman would die at the loss of a few drops of blood.

But Robin smiled faintly where he lay. "Mine own dear Little John," whispered he, "heaven bless thy kind, rough heart. But we will never roam the woodlands together again."

"Aye, but we will!" quoth Little John loudly. "No more harm shall come upon thee! Am I not by? Let me see who dares touch—" Here he stopped of a sudden, for his words choked him. At last he said, in a husky voice, "Now, if aught of harm befalls thee because of this day's doings, I swear by Saint George that hot flames shall lick every crack and cranny of this house. As for these women—it will be an ill day for them!"

But Robin Hood took Little John's rough, brown fist in his white hands, and chid him softly, asking him since what time Little John had thought of doing harm to women, even in vengeance. Thus he talked till at last the other promised that no ill should fall upon the place, no matter what happened. Then a silence fell, and Little John sat with Robin's hand in his. The sun dropped slowly to the west, till all the sky was ablaze with a red glory. Then Robin Hood, in a faltering voice, bade Little John raise him, that he might look out once more upon the woodlands; so the yeoman lifted him in his arms, and Robin's head lay on his friend's shoulder. Long he gazed, while the other sat with bowed head, the hot tears rolling from his eyes, for he felt that the time of parting was near at hand. Presently, Robin Hood bade him string his stout bow for him, and choose a smooth fair arrow from his quiver. This Little John did, though without disturbing his master or rising from where he sat. Robin Hood's fingers wrapped lovingly around his bow, and he smiled faintly when he felt it in his grasp; then he nocked the arrow. "Little John," said he, "mine own dear friend, mark, I prithee, where this arrow lodges, and there let my grave be digged. Lay me with my face toward the east, Little John, and see that my resting place be kept green, and that my weary bones be not disturbed."

As he finished speaking, he raised himself of a sudden and sat upright. His old strength seemed to come back to him, and, drawing the bowstring to his ear, he sped the arrow out the open casement. As the shaft flew, his hand sank slowly with the bow till it lay across his knees, and his body likewise sank back again into Little John's loving arms; but something had sped from that body, even as the winged arrow sped from the bow.

For some minutes Little John sat motionless, but presently he laid that which he held gently down, then, folding the hands upon the breast and covering up the face, he turned upon his heel and left the room without a word or a sound.

Upon the steep stairway he met the Prioress and some of the chief among the sisters. To them he said in a deep, quivering voice, "An ye go within a score of feet of yonder room, I will tear down your rookery over your heads so that not one stone shall be left upon another." So saying, he left them, and they presently saw him running across the open, through the falling of the dusk, until he was swallowed up by the forest.

The early gray of the coming morn was just beginning to lighten the black sky toward the eastward when Little John and six more of the band came rapidly across the open toward the nunnery. They saw no one, for the sisters were all hidden away from sight. Up the stone stair they ran, and a great sound of weeping was presently heard. After a while this ceased, and then came the scuffling and shuffling of men's feet as they carried a heavy weight down the steep and winding stairs. So they went forth from the nunnery, and, as they passed through the doors thereof, a great, loud sound of wailing arose from the glade that lay all dark in the dawning, as though many men, hidden in the shadows, had lifted up their voices in sorrow.

Thus died Robin Hood, at Kirklees Nunnery, with mercy in his heart toward those that had been his undoing; for thus he showed pity for the weak through all the time of his living.

His yeomen were scattered henceforth, but no great ill befell them thereafter, for, a more merciful sheriff succeeding the one that had gone, and they being separated here and there throughout the countryside, they abided in peace and quietness, so that many lived to hand down these tales to their children and their children's children.

A certain one sayeth that upon a stone at Kirklees is an old inscription. This I give in the ancient English in which it was written, and thus it runs:

> *Hear undernead dis laitl stean*
> *Lais Robert Earl of Huntingtun*
> *Nea arcir ver as hie sae geud*
> *An pipl kauld im Robin Heud*
> *Sick utlaws as hi an is men*
> *Vil England nidir si agen.*
> *Obiit 24 Kal. Dekembris 1247.*

And now, dear friend, we also must part, for our merry journeyings have ended, and here, at the grave of Robin Hood, we turn, each going his own way.

Howard Pyle
(1853–1911)

FROM A BOY enchanted by legends of the Round Table, buccaneers, and daring adventure, Howard Pyle grew to become a writer and illustrator whose stories of King Arthur and Robin Hood still delight young readers today. Pyle was born March 5, 1853, in Wilmington, Delaware, to a family of Quakers. As well as having a passion for legends, he learned about the power of illustration during the Civil War, when periodicals offered compelling pictorials of action on the front lines.

His preference for the magical regions of the imagination over the mundane demands of the "three R's" led to lackluster performance in school. His parents sent him to a Pennsylvania boarding school in hopes of improving his academic standing, with little success. Since his grades were not good enough for acceptance to college, his parents acceded to his wishes and sent him to art school.

At the Philadelphia Academy of Professor Van Der Veilen, Pyle finally excelled in a course of study of drawing, painting, and composition. The art instruction of the day consisted primarily of studying and copying the works of "masters," and Pyle was not prepared to earn a living from his art. After graduating in 1872, he returned to Wilmington to work in his father's leather business. Years later, Pyle recalled this period, noting "the hardest thing for a student to do after leaving an art school is to adapt the knowledge there gained to practical use—to do creative work, for the work in an art school is imitative. When I left art school I discovered, like many others, that I could not easily train myself to creative work."

Pyle's first commercial success came in 1876. Inspired by the atmosphere of the tiny island of Chincoteague off the Virginia coast, Pyle wrote and illustrated a tale about an aging, bitter parson who swallows a magic pill and is transformed into a young boy. He sent the story to *Scribner's Magazine*, which accepted it at once.

In mid-October, Pyle went to New York City, determined to work as an illustrator. Portfolio in hand, he went door to door, calling on the art directors of major periodicals. He was undeterred by the initial rejections, and his persistence paid off when, within a month, he had a seventy-five-dollar commission from *St. Nicholas*, a popular magazine for children. Soon Pyle joined the staff of *Harper's*, which provided him with a practical education in the wood engraving techniques essential to the illustration process of his day.

For all his apparent professional good fortune, Pyle had a difficult time convincing art directors that he was craftsman enough to submit final drawings for engraving. He devoted himself to mastering the subtleties of tone and shading, and a year following his arrival in New York, a piece entitled "A Wreck in the Offing" was accepted by *Harper's*.

In late 1879, he returned to Wilmington to enjoy the company of his family and his beloved countryside. In spite of being removed from the publishing circles of the city, Pyle's reputation continued to grow and his illustrated story "Old Times in a Quaker Town" received national attention. With his career well established, Pyle felt secure enough to marry Anne Poole in 1881. They had six children.

By 1883, Pyle completed *The Merry Adventures of Robin Hood*, which he illustrated and retold for the modern ear. It was released simultaneously in Britain and America, and garnered critical acclaim on both sides of the Atlantic. He also wrote and illustrated his first original novel in 1885, *Within the Capes*, soon followed by *The Wonderful Clock*, and *Otto of the Silver Hand*.

Despite a generous output of novels, fairy tales, and illustrations, Pyle's creative ambitions were not satisfied. In 1894, he accepted a teaching post at the Drexel Institute of Arts and Sciences in Philadelphia. His classes were enormously popular, attracting students from around the country. Feeling constrained by the philosophy of the institute, which favored technique over the imagination, Pyle left Drexel to found the Brandywine School. The curriculum at Brandywine was rigorous, requiring a year-round commitment from its students, who resided in Wilmington for the school year and at Chadds Ford, Pyle's country home, during the summer months. Pyle's students included N. C. Wyeth and Maxfield Parrish, both of whom became artists of great commercial success and influence.

As well as running the school, Pyle continued his own work. Describing Pyle's genius for juggling tasks, former student Thomas Oakley recalled, "On the stairway landing I found my teacher at his easel, working on a canvas, his young children cavorting about his knees, a model posed nearby in costume to give him some detail of texture, Mrs. Pyle sitting beside him, reading aloud proofs from *King Arthur* for his correction, he making comments for her notation."

Although Pyle had set the standard for American illustration in the latter 1800s, by the turn of the century technology was changing, permitting different modes of illustration, which created new styles and new stars. Pyle returned to working with children's classics. For nearly ten years, he was absorbed by his work on the legends of King Arthur's Round Table. His retelling constituted four volumes, and is still in print.

During his final years, Pyle turned his attention to mural making. He took his family to Italy so he could study the Italian masters. At the outset of the journey, he was stricken with kidney disease. He died in Florence four months later in the spring of 1911, at the age of 58.

Other Titles by Howard Pyle

Empty Bottles. Rochester, NY: Rochester Folk Art Press, 1975.

King Stork. (illus.) Boston: Little, Brown, 1986.

The Merry Adventures of Robin Hood. New York: Scribners, 1946.

Otto of the Silver Hand. New York: Dover Press, 1967.

Sixth Merry Adventure of Robin Hood. New York: Dover Press, 1986.

The Story of King Arthur and His Knights. New York: Scribners, 1984.

The Story of Sir Launcelot and His Companions. New York: Scribners, 1985.

The Story of the Champions of the Round Table. New York: Scribners, 1984.

The Story of the Grail and the Passing of Arthur. New York: Scribners, 1985.

The Wonder Clock, or *Four and Twenty Marvelous Tales, Being One for Each Hour of the Day*. New York: Dover Press, 1970.